SIX-GUN JUSTICE

Rachel stood with his spare Colt in her hand. She had
fished it out of his saddlebags. He tried to remember if it
had been loaded. Slocum did not think so. Rachel had
retrieved his six-shooter, loaded it and then had used it
methodically on her attacker.

From the way the woman held the gun, it was not the
first time she had fired a six-gun.

"Thought you were dead," she said simply. Rachel lowered the hammer on the Colt. Slocum realized then how
close he had come to taking a round from his own spare
six-shooter. She swung the pistol around and handed it
butt first to him.

Slocum took it without saying a word.

He turned from the impassive woman and knelt by the
man all curled up in a ball on the ground. Slocum rolled
the man over. The clouds above parted just enough to cast
a ray of cold silver moonlight on the man's face.

Slocum looked up at Rachel and said, "You killed Larson."

"Fancy that," was all she said.

D1407809

JAKE LOGAN

SLOCUM
AND THE AMBUSH TRAIL

JOVE BOOKS, NEW YORK

This is a work of fiction. Names, characters, places, and incidents are either the product of the author's imagination or are used fictitiously, and any resemblance to actual persons, living or dead, business establishments, events, or locales is entirely coincidental.

SLOCUM AND THE AMBUSH TRAIL

A Jove Book / published by arrangement with
the author

PRINTING HISTORY
Jove edition / December 2000

The Penguin Putnam Inc. World Wide Web site address is
http://www.penguinputnam.com

ISBN: 0-515-12976-3

A JOVE BOOK®
Jove Books are published by The Berkley Publishing Group,
a division of Penguin Putnam Inc.,
375 Hudson Street, New York, New York 10014.
JOVE and the "J" design
are trademarks belonging to Penguin Putnam Inc.

PRINTED IN THE UNITED STATES OF AMERICA

10 9 8 7 6 5 4 3 2 1

1

It took John Slocum more than an hour to come to a decision. He pushed back from the bar just off Larrimer Square in Denver, settled his gun belt with the ebony-handled Colt Navy slung cross-draw style, then tried not to look too eager as he strolled to the poker table. Four men sat there, cards clutched close to their chests as though the pounding of their hearts might increase their chances of winning.

If wishes were carriages, these gents would be riding in style.

Slocum had seen how they played and knew the lot of them were rank amateurs. Just the kind of poker players he appreciated most—because they were easily separated from their money, and he had very little of that riding in his shirt pocket.

"You gents mind if I sit in?" Slocum asked. His green eyes darted around the table, taking in the four men. He stood better than six feet tall and dominated them. Not a one was within inches as tall. Sitting down so they had to peer up at him, they were even more easily cowed, all except one who had the look of a long trail drive about him. He had the biggest stack of chips in front of him and was the one Slocum figured he could clean out within a few hands.

"We got a spare chair jist waitin' fer ya," said the drover with the chips Slocum hankered after. He pointed. As he did so, he almost knocked over the half-full whiskey bottle on the table. He had imbibed a considerable portion of the rotgut, making Slocum even more eager to join the game. A man with a snoot full of whiskey made bad decisions and, even when relatively sober, he had not played all that well.

Still, Slocum had seen men whose luck improved the drunker they got. God watched out for fools and drunks. He wasn't sure if he wasn't going to be playing both tonight.

"Thank you," Slocum said, scooting the chair back, throwing his leg over it and sitting. The rickety wood chair groaned under his weight. He hardly noticed that or anything else around him now. The smoke-filled saloon vanished. The pretty waitress girls flitting about, selling drinks and stealing cowboys' money vanished. Even the stench of spilled beer and whiskey not worth putting a match to disappeared. All that remained were the pasteboard cards, the stained, green felt table and the four men Slocum wanted to beat.

He had been on the trail for well nigh a month by the time he rode into Denver from the wilds of Wyoming. He wasn't much for crowds, and Denver had become a mighty big town, booming from silver strikes across the mountains in Leadville along the California Gulch and even as far south as Cripple Creek. Denver supplied the miners with the goods needed to keep them alive and was awash in money. Slocum cared little for the people; having been broke for almost three months and living off the land made him very appreciative of the easy money to be had in a card game with poor gamblers.

"What's your pleasure?" asked the man across from

him. Slocum eyed him closer. He had thought the man to be a drover. He changed his opinion just a little. The man had been on the trail a long time but not herding cattle. A scout? Or something to do with a wagon train? He had the harsh look of a mule skinner about him, down to the powerful hands and squinty eyes. Slocum could imagine him expertly cracking a twenty-foot-long whip to get a balky team moving.

"Seven card stud?" Slocum asked, looking around to see if anyone objected. No one did.

"Well, that's jist fine with me, too," the mule skinner said. "My name's Voss, and I aim to clean you out, mister."

"Slocum's mine, and it looks like we got similar goals," Slocum said, smiling. The hiss of the cards coming off the deck and sliding around the table occupied Slocum for the next few minutes. His luck ran about what it had for the prior three months; the best he got was a pair of kings, which lost to Voss's three deuces.

Then Slocum found his stride. The others drank more heavily. He only sipped at the whiskey, preferring to keep a clear head. When one of the scantily clad, pretty waitress girls came by the table, Slocum pushed across a crumpled ten-dollar greenback to her for another bottle. He wanted his newfound companions to enjoy themselves—before he wiped them out.

That bottle of trade whiskey was about a quarter gone when the first of the men went bust, all his money now in front of Slocum. Before the bottle was only half-filled with its amber liquid, the game was between Slocum and Voss.

"You're a mighty good player, Slocum," Voss said. "But I'm better."

"My pile of chips says you're not," Slocum replied, smiling a little to take the edge off his words. He was keyed up now. He had won over a hundred dollars. If he walked away with Voss's stash, it would more than make up for the lean times he had gone through. He might see as much as five hundred dollars. Not a bad night's work, and it was legal.

"Draw poker for a spell?" suggested Voss.

"The game doesn't matter to me. I can beat you at high-low or anything else." Slocum watched as Voss shuffled the deck. With the man's strong, pudgy fingers, he was not likely to manipulate the deck like some tinhorn gambler. But Slocum was taking no chances now. He saw the deal was honest, no seconds dealt or a special card slipped off the bottom.

He drew the cards to him and tried not to look surprised. He had four tens. This was good and bad. If he didn't ask for any cards, it might scare Voss off. If he asked for only one card, he could not improve his hand but might lure Voss into thinking he had a busted flush and was bluffing.

"Well, well, lookee here," Voss said, grinning ear to ear. "I been waitin' my whole danged life for a hand like this."

Slocum said nothing. He had seen Voss bluff earlier. He had seen Voss with a winning hand. But now he could not tell which the mule skinner held. In spite of the whiskey, the amount of money riding on the turn of these cards had sobered Voss and turned him into a better card player.

"Good enough to bet, say, a hundred dollars?" asked Slocum. He pushed the money to the center of the table. A hush fell around the table. This was a big pot and likely to get bigger, unless Voss folded. A small crowd gathered, then pushed closer when Voss saw Slocum's hundred and raised another hundred.

"How many cards you wantin', Slocum? All five?" laughed Voss. His fingers tapped on the deck. Nerves. Slocum thought the man was bluffing, so he did a bit of playacting on his own. He licked his lips and let his eyes dance around the circle of onlookers, as if begging them for some bit of luck.

"One," Slocum said, sliding his lone card out. He hurriedly scooped up the one Voss gave him and let his face flash a brief, if phony, irritation. Then he squared the cards on the table in front of him and smiled.

"So?" asked Voss.

"How many you taking?"

"I'll stand with these. How can I beat perfection? How can *you* beat perfection?" asked the mule skinner.

"I'm kicking in another hundred," said Slocum. "No, let's make that two hundred."

"Now, Slocum, I think you're bluffing. That card you got didn't finish off a straight, didn't help you one little bit on a flush, didn't do nuthin' for you. I'll raise you . . . five hundred."

Slocum frowned, then said, "You don't have five hundred. You can't even see one hundred."

"Well, now, Slocum, I got a mighty fine wagon loaded with cargo outside of town, over near Auraria, that's worth more. I'll pledge that, because I don't think you've got squat."

"How do I know this wagon and its cargo is worth the dynamite it would take to blow it up?"

"If you want to back down, say so," Voss said. The onlookers laughed at this.

"Everything," Slocum said, pushing his entire pile forward. "Let me see a bill of sale on your wagon and the cargo."

Voss hiccuped, then leaned forward and rummaged in a vest pocket before pulling out a rumpled piece of paper.

"This here's good enough, I reckon. I'll sign it over to you—if you win. Which you won't."

Slocum took the scrap of paper and looked at the smeared, almost illegible print. It was a bill of sale made out to Voss giving him the wagon and a yoke of oxen.

"Doesn't say anything about the cargo."

"Lemme add that, then." Voss snickered and Slocum wondered why.

"Show me your cards," Slocum said. He stood to lose everything if he had read Voss wrong, yet he felt nothing. It was as if ice water had started pumping through his veins. No nerves, no sense of anticipation. Whatever came, he was ready for it.

"Look at 'em and weep," Voss said, fanning out the cards. "A baby straight, twos through sixes." He grinned, showing a broken tooth in front. He reached for the pot.

Slocum stopped him.

"Four tens."

For a moment utter silence descended on the saloon, then a loud cheer went up. Voss turned pale under his weathered exterior.

"No, you were bluffin'. I saw it in your eyes. You couldn't have—" The truth set in, and Voss turned even paler. His hands shook, and he licked his lips nervously. "You can't take the wagon. You can't take the cargo. Please, Slocum."

"You bet, you lost," Slocum said. "Sign at the bottom. I'm the new owner of a wagon, team and all the cargo."

"You don't know what you're doin'," Voss pleaded. "I *got* to get that cargo across the Front Range to Leadville. I *want* to!"

Slocum didn't understand that, but he did know he had won and had dozens of witnesses.

"Sign everything over to me." From someone in the crowd came a pencil. It rattled on the table between Slocum and Voss. "Now," Slocum said with steely determination. He had no reason to shepherd a rig across Mosquito Pass into Leadville. Finding a buyer in Denver would be easier. Let someone whose business was freighting collect a few dollars delivering cases of beans or sides of beef—whatever Voss had been contracted to deliver.

Still, Slocum wondered at the freighter's peculiar statement about *wanting* to deliver the cargo.

"You're a cowboy. You got the look about you, Slocum. Don't take the wagon. It's all I got."

"You want to buy it back?" Slocum asked. "Five hundred dollars sounds like a fair price."

"But the cargo's worth ten times that!" Voss blurted.

Only Slocum heard. The rest of the saloon patrons had drifted away in search of other entertainment. Several Cyprians came down from cribs on the second floor, offering themselves at bargain prices. Those that weren't drunk enough avoided them, preferring to get even more inebriated before crawling up next to such ugly women.

Voss's exclamation piqued Slocum's curiosity.

"What's worth five thousand dollars? You couldn't pack that much gold into a single wagon—and why take gold to Leadville?"

"Not gold. Something more valuable. Please, Slocum," the mule skinner begged.

"Reckon I want to see what I just won," Slocum said, standing. Voss jumped up on unsteady legs. The whiskey was getting to him now, that and torment over having lost his livelihood.

Slocum left the saloon and stepped into the bracing cold Denver night. Stars shone like diamonds above, and a trace of wind whipped down off the Front Range carrying promise of an early winter. It was only mid-September, but snow might come at any time, especially up in the higher elevations.

He turned when Voss grabbed his arm.

"Slocum, I'm beggin' you! Don't take the wagon."

"What's your cargo?" Slocum asked, still wondering at what Voss had said. Any regular shipment might be valuable, but not that valuable. Dynamite? Freighters took it through Mosquito Pass all the time for the miners in Leadville. Food? Whiskey? Good money could be made, but it was risky getting over the mountains and would not fetch such a princely sum as five thousand dollars.

Not a single wagonload.

"I . . . please," sobbed Voss. This was not the response Slocum had expected from a hard-bitten trailsman like Voss.

"Let's check the cargo, then I'll make a decision." Slocum read the man like a bold newspaper headline. Voss did not want Slocum to even see the cargo. He got to his horse, Voss trailing behind and almost blubbering. The freighter was getting on Slocum's nerves, and he told Voss so.

"You don't know what this means to me, Slocum."

"I know you lost at poker." Slocum rode off, leaving Voss behind. He heard the man's boots pounding on the Denver street and then a galloping horse coming up from behind. Voss shot past him, obviously thinking to outleg Slocum and reach the wagon with its mysterious cargo before him. Slocum picked up the pace a little, not pushing his horse. Let Voss kill his horse galloping like that all the way to Auraria across Cherry Creek.

Slocum followed at a more leisurely walk and arrived at a muddy field where a dozen tents had been pitched amid a passel of wagons. Spotting Voss was not hard. He had dropped from his exhausted horse and started toward a Conestoga wagon with a tattered canvas top. Slocum shook his head. For getting across the prairie, this was a fine choice. But to take it up narrow mountain roads was another matter entirely. The double team of oxen might be up to the chore, but the width of the wagon bed made getting through some tight spots in the trail arduous and maybe even impossible.

It was about what he expected from Voss.

Slocum dismounted and started after the freighter when he saw a man with a bandanna pulled up over his face step out from behind a large tent. A campfire illuminated the drawn six-shooter in his hand.

"Voss, Voss!" shouted Slocum. "Look out!"

The freighter skidded to a halt, turned and caught the masked man's round smack in the center of his chest. If Slocum had not warned Voss, he might have been gunned down from behind. Either way turned out the same. Voss died fast.

Slocum's hand flew to his cross-draw holster. The Colt Navy swung out in a smooth, well-practiced motion, and he fired three times at the masked killer. His rounds missed, but he drove off the bushwhacker. Slocum dodged among the tents and wagons, chasing the killer.

All around, men and women stirred, roused by the gunfire. Slocum yelled to stop the fleeing murderer, but no one felt brave enough to interfere. Slocum ran hard, looked for a clean shot at Voss's assailant, and saw he was falling farther and farther behind. The man ran like a deer, jumping fires and agilely avoiding boxes and other debris scattered around the field.

Slocum skidded to a halt, lifted his six-shooter and aimed the best he could in the darkness. His pistol spat lead. During the war he had been a sniper, one of the most skillful, and knew instinctively when a shot was good. This had not been a killing shot, but he had hit his target. Slocum resumed his pursuit and saw a patch of blood already turning the dirt into gory mud.

He looked around but saw nothing. The wounded killer had gone to ground. Slocum's chances of finding him in the field dotted with tents and wagons was close to nothing. He reluctantly accepted the odds and knew it was time to fold. Finding the dry-gulching son of a bitch he had winged would be a chore for a posse, not a single man. Shoving his six-gun back into the holster, Slocum retraced his steps. Voss lay staring up at the sky where he had been shot. No one had come to see if the man was dead or alive.

Slocum checked, although his gut told him the truth before he verified it. Voss was stone-cold dead. Slocum looked up at the wagon some distance away that Voss had been running toward and decided that was what he now held title to. He took a deep breath and walked the twenty yards to the wagon.

He fumbled untying the leather thongs holding the back flap in place, then pulled the canvas away to see what Voss coveted so. For a moment, Slocum failed to understand what was going on. Then it came to him in a rush.

"What are you staring at, mister? Haven't you ever seen a woman before?"

Slocum said nothing. The lovely redhead speaking to him so sarcastically ignored the other three even prettier women stretched out on pallets in the wagon bed, awakened from their sleep by his unmannerly intrusion.

2

"You going to gawk at us all night or are you going to do the gentlemanly thing and close that flap so we can have some privacy?" The red-haired woman's lips thinned to a determined line as she looked ready to grab something and fling it at Slocum.

"I didn't mean to disturb you," Slocum said.

"Then get out and let us be!"

"This *is* Voss's wagon?" Slocum asked, wondering if he had made a mistake. Deep in his gut he didn't think so. If these four women were Voss's cargo, that explained why the man was so unnerved at losing them in a poker game. Slocum still needed an explanation of why Voss had four beautiful women, looking to be in their early twenties and as different as they could be, in a wagon headed over the mountains.

Unless . . .

A shiver ran up and down Slocum's spine.

"You're mail-order brides," he said.

"Give that man a cigar," spoke up another of the women, a woman with light blond hair and dancing blue eyes. "In fact, Maggie, I'm willing to give him a lot more than that."

"Shut up, Comfort, and keep those legs of yours closed tight. If you can," the redhead said.

"I know two of your names now," Slocum said, facing down Maggie. The redhead glared at him, then turned and snapped at Comfort.

"You talk too much."

"Aw, Maggie, this is an adventure. You can't have an adventure if you don't *enjoy* it. Every little bit of it."

"Bet it is little, too," grumbled the dark-haired woman at the front of the wagon. She pulled her blanket up tightly around her chin and stared at Slocum. He tried to read her expression but couldn't. She had been sarcastic, but not like Maggie, and seemed to hold no animosity toward him like Maggie. He was beside himself trying to figure out what was going on.

"I'm John Slocum," he introduced.

"And you're going to get the hell out of here, John Slocum, or I'll call the law!"

"Might be a good idea," Slocum said, "since Voss got himself shot down not sixty feet from this wagon."

"What?" This produced the first spark of interest from the brunette. Her eyes went wide and a hand flew to her mouth. "What happened?"

"Hush, Elizabeth, I'll handle this." Maggie ruled the roost like a mother hen, although she might not have been as old as Elizabeth. A year or two could matter a great deal on the frontier when it came to experience.

Slocum tried to figure out what was going on with the women. They were beautiful and ought to have had no trouble finding husbands back East or wherever they hailed from. Their personalities varied as much as their looks. Redheaded Maggie was a firebrand, matching her locks with a snappish manner that would put off most men. Elizabeth's brown hair fell in soft waves to her shoulders, and she had been withdrawn and disinterested until Slocum mentioned that Voss had been cut down. He wondered if she and the freighter had been more than just friends. Still boldly appraising him, Comfort allowed her blanket to fall to her waist. Big breasts tried to force their way through her thin nightgown in an obvious attempt to lure him.

Comfort wanted adventure. She was likely to find more than she could handle if she came on to all men like this, Slocum thought.

The other woman, the dark-haired one, chewed on her lower lip and appeared worried about everything. She spoke when Slocum made no move to leave.

"Does this sort of thing happen often?" she asked. "This is terribly frightening."

"I'll take care of it, Rachel," Maggie cut in. "You all stay quiet now and let me handle him."

"You always get all the fun," Comfort said. "*I* want to handle him, too. That sounds like a barrel of fun. Doesn't it to you, John?" She grinned ear to ear, and Slocum swallowed hard. Comfort had twisted just enough to give him a flash of her snowy white bare breast. He had been on the trail too long, and it must have been a year since he had seen any women even half as lovely as these. The whores in the saloon where he had won the wagon—and the four women—from Voss had been as ugly as sin.

"What's this you said about Voss being injured?" Maggie demanded.

"Didn't say injured. Meant dead. A masked man walked up and pumped lead into him. I chased the killer and winged him, then lost him in the camp." Slocum glanced over his shoulder. "What is this place, anyway?"

"We're preparing to go over the Front Range to Leadville," Elizabeth said. She smiled almost shyly. "We're looking for rich husbands."

"Miners?" Slocum hardly believed his ears.

"Millionaires are made every day in Leadville," Maggie said tartly. "We want our share."

"So you'll marry a grizzled miner with more money than teeth?" Slocum shook his head.

"I don't suppose you'd like to audition for *my* husband, would you?" asked Comfort.

The other three women glared at her, but the blonde ignored them. She licked her lips and batted her long eyelashes in Slocum's direction.

"Sorry, ma'am," Slocum said. "I'm not a rich miner." Truth was, he felt rich with all the money riding in his pocket. He had not bothered to count it, but he had to be six hundred dollars to the good.

And he owned this wagon and the cargo in it. If anyone could ever own a human being. Slocum had gone through the war debating that problem with himself and had come to the conclusion that the Yankee slogan "Live free or die" was the best way to live, man or woman, white or black. He might own the wagon these women rode in but he had no claim on them. Voss obviously thought he did own them from the way he talked.

"Even if you're not a rich miner, maybe you can make my night a little more exciting," Comfort offered.

"We got some business to work out," Slocum said, directing his words to Maggie. She seemed the best one to deal with. "Voss is dead, but he lost this wagon to me in a poker game a couple hours ago."

"Maggie, maybe he killed Mr. Voss and stole the papers," Rachel said in a flat voice.

"There's a whole saloon full of men who watched the game." Slocum pulled out the bill of sale and handed it to Maggie. She peered at it, then moved the paper closer to the kerosene lamp in the middle of the wagon. The redhead got to the end of the page, then started all over again. She tossed the scrap of paper back to Slocum.

"That looks like Voss's hen scratching," she said. "It doesn't matter much if he's dead or not. Slocum is the owner of this wagon."

"Voss said the cargo came with it," Slocum said.

"But *we're* the cargo," protested Elizabeth. "Are you going to take us over the Front Range, Mr. Slocum? Mr. Voss said it was a dangerous trip and only experienced freighters could make the trip through Mosquito Pass."

"He was right on that," Slocum admitted. "Don't rightly know how he intended to get a Conestoga through some of the narrow parts of the trail. Even with six oxen in front of this wagon, getting over the pass is not going to be a picnic." He wondered what the wagon and yoke of oxen might fetch. Voss had overestimated their value, but Slocum had already figured that out when he allowed the wagon master to put up the title to the rig.

To the rig and cargo.

Slocum had expected foodstuffs, gunpowder, luxury items the miners would pay exorbitant prices for. He had not expected to find four women calling themselves the cargo.

"But you will see us to Leadville, won't you, Mr. Slocum?" asked Elizabeth. She brushed back her brown hair. She was another hothouse flower thrust out onto the trail, he saw. Her pale face had sunburned in places, causing some skin to peel. In spite of this, she was exquisite, the most beautiful of the four beautiful women.

"Can't say I will," he answered. "I don't know what you paid Voss for the trip, but that contract died with him. I own the wagon, and if I can find someone to buy it, I will. Perhaps you can dicker with them and get over the mountains. This time of year, you have to be careful and travel fast so you won't get caught in an early storm. Get stranded up there and you'll die. Even experienced hunters and mountain men die."

"Wait a minute, Slocum," demanded Maggie when he started to pull down the canvas flap and let them be. "You won this wagon."

"I did."

"Then you won Voss's obligations, too. We paid him to take us over the mountains. You have to honor that."

"Why are you so all-fired intent on going to Leadville to find husbands?" he asked, curious. "Stay in Denver. Find yourselves merchants. They might not be as ... exciting," he said, looking at Comfort, "but the life here is a lot more comfortable than on the other side of the mountains, even with a rich miner."

From what Slocum had seen of boomtowns, the miners did little but die in unsavory conditions. The mine owners seldom stayed in the boomtowns, preferring more civilized locales—such as Denver. The ones who profited most, usually including the mine owners, were those tireless men who sold supplies. Horace Tabor had become wildly rich supplying prospectors, taking a share of any find as payment. His own ventures into exploration had been busts, even buying property from a crook named Chicken Bill that had been salted. That was the type of man these women ought to be looking for rather than grimy miners with wheezing lungs and bowed backs from crawling in too-low tunnels.

The only reason he could think these four wanted to marry a miner was the short life span of a man hidden away a mile underground, using explosives and that soul-destroying, body-ruining piece of mining equipment called a "widow maker." Marry well, lose the husband to an accident, then move on with a mountain of money.

Slocum did not know the women, other than from the brief few minutes he had spoken with them, but they did not seem to be gold diggers. Comfort, perhaps, but not withdrawn Rachel or Elizabeth or even cantankerous Maggie. Still, he made a good deal of his money gambling. Slocum had learned to size up a man fast from across a poker table. There were undercurrents with these women he did not understand, but the story of going to

Leadville to marry wealthy prospectors flew in the face of all he thought he knew of them.

He shook his head sadly. He really knew nothing of them. Maybe they *were* all gold diggers. What did he know? What did he care?

"Why don't we discuss the matter in the morning?" Slocum said. "I want to find the law and take care of Voss's body before it starts to smell too bad."

Rachel turned away. Elizabeth put her hand to her mouth. Comfort lost some of her friskiness and even Maggie appeared distressed over the implications of the freighter being murdered.

Slocum lowered the flap, wondering what the hell he was going to do. Nursemaiding the four over one of the most rugged passes in the territory was out of the question. Slocum wanted to relax and enjoy everything Denver had to offer, though from the way Comfort had been giving him the eye he could do a lot worse back in town. Slocum shook off the notion that he ought to listen, even for a minute, to their pleas about taking them to Leadville.

Someone in the camp would want the wagon and team of oxen, even if Slocum had to take a fire-sale price for them. Better to be a few dollars ahead than to be trapped in the middle of Mosquito Pass during an early snowstorm with four women who looked out of place even in Auraria. In the mountains, they would be worse than out of place—they would be a hindrance that might kill him.

Slocum walked to Voss's body and stared at the freighter. "You sorry son of a bitch," Slocum said softly. "What did you get yourself into?" He set off to find a policeman or special or whatever the town called their lawmen. Reporting the murder would cause a ruckus, but Slocum felt he owed it to Voss. He might even see the man got a decent funeral if Auraria was going to put him away in some potter's field, as was likely.

Going to his horse, Slocum put his foot in the stirrup

and prepared to mount when the hair on the back of his neck stood on end. He dropped back to the ground and half turned, his hand on the butt of his Colt Navy. Standing a few yards away in shadows was a man watching him like a snake watches a bird.

"Anything I can do for you?" Slocum asked.

"Didn't think you spotted me," the man said in a gravelly voice. "Since you ask, there is something."

Slocum settled his nerves. This felt like a showdown, and he was ready to draw.

The man stepped out of the shadows, favoring one leg just a mite. The dim light from the stars did little to illuminate his face, but Slocum doubted he had never met the man before now. There was something just a tad familiar about the way he stood and talked, but the man might have been any of a hundred other gunfighters Slocum had crossed trails with in his time.

"My name's Larson, and I was wonderin' what you was doin' talkin' to the women in that wagon yonder."

"I own the wagon," Slocum said.

"No, no you don't. That's *my* wagon, and those women are *my* property. You go nosin' around my property anymore, and I'll cut that snout of yours off!"

Slocum faced the man squarely. Larson had seen his share of fights. His forehead looked like a road map crisscrossed with no fewer than a half dozen pink scars, maybe from knife fights, possibly from bullets almost going through his head. Larson's eyes were cold, dark and flat, without emotion. Slocum had seen stone killers in his day. Larson was another.

"Prove it," Slocum said.

"I don't have to. You stay away and—"

"And nothing," Slocum cut him off. "I own the wagon. I own the wagon and the oxen, but I surely do not own the women. And neither do you."

"Now ain't you the abolitionist?" sneered Larson.

Slocum had fought for the Confederacy and had worked out what he really thought about slavery. His family in Calhoun, Georgia, had never owned slaves, and he was not going to pretend he owned those women. They were not property. He let Larson know it in no uncertain terms.

Slocum judged distances and unloaded a roundhouse punch that ended smack in the middle of Larson's face. The man grunted, stumbled backward, then let out a yowl of pain.

"You busted my nose!"

"Might improve your looks," Slocum said coldly. "And maybe it'll help your memory about who really owns the wagon—and who doesn't own the women."

"You, you'll pay for this!" Larson held his hand to his gushing nose and stumbled off into the night, muttering curses as he went. Slocum watched him go, wondering what that had been about. Had Larson thought to scare him away that easily? Slocum was too tired to care about the man or his motives. Denver was a boomtown filled with confidence men of all stripes. Larson might have overheard some of the conversation with the women, or he might have mistaken Slocum for Voss, although Slocum doubted Voss would have backed down, either, in the face of such a ridiculous claim.

Larson may somehow have learned of Voss's death and thought to take advantage of an opportunity. The killing had been public enough, even if no one took notice. It had been Larson's misfortune he had crossed John Slocum and not some tenderfoot unwilling to stand up to him.

Slocum mounted and rode toward a cluster of buildings a mile off, hunting for the sheriff or marshal or whoever could deal with Voss's murder.

It did not surprise him when the lawman was less than interested in the death and far from eager about tracking down Voss's killer.

3

Slocum stood at the edge of the field where the wagons rested and the others looking to make their fortunes in the silver fields of Leadville stirred to face a new day. He shook his head. Years back, he had worked in a mine and knew that the backbreaking toil seldom delivered the bounty these poor fools thought would be theirs. Still, most of the men sought the precious metals while the four women in the Conestoga sought something else—miners already possessed of the metal.

Such lovely women only doomed themselves. Why they had ventured to Colorado Territory rather than staying in their safe cities was beyond him. Comfort had given him the come-hither look of a woman on the prowl. She had said more than once that she sought adventure. Slocum thought that was fair enough, but he hardly considered struggling to fix some grimy miner's meals and tend his shack—or even his home—to be much of an adventure. Rachel was the kind to avoid adventure, if he read her right. And Maggie? She could have come to the top no matter where she was. Why did she herd the others toward Leadville like a sheepdog tending a flock?

The one who caught his eye, though, was Elizabeth.

She had only a fraction of the fire and grit Maggie showed, but there was a determination in her he saw immediately. Elizabeth struck him as levelheaded and not the kind to go off like Comfort, hunting for elusive thrills.

All in all, the four were a strange cargo headed for Leadville. Slocum was not sure he wished them the best toward reaching their goal, but he certainly wished them no harm. He hitched up his gun belt and started across the field, wending his way through new cooking fires and men tending their equipment in preparation for starting their trip over the Front Range into the silver fields.

Slocum's pace quickened when he saw Maggie, Rachel and Comfort clinging to one another. Rachel cried openly. Comfort looked frightened and Maggie mad as a wet hen.

"What's wrong?" he called as he rushed to them.

"What do you care?" the redhead snapped. "You're going to sell the wagon out from under us."

"What's wrong?" he asked again, aiming the question at Comfort. Rachel cried too hard to answer coherently. The blonde shook her head and tried to force out the words.

"She . . . she's gone, taken."

"Elizabeth?"

"As if you cared a whit," Maggie said angrily. "For all we know, you might be the one who kidnapped her. Maybe you're going to sell her into slavery at one of those whorehouses you were going on about. Isn't that where you won the wagon and team from Voss? At a whorehouse?"

"Who kidnapped her?" Slocum asked.

"How the hell should we know?"

"Has there been a ransom demand?" Rachel shook her head while the other two just stared at him. Slocum took this to mean there had not been a note. "Then how do you know she didn't just wander off? Or maybe she chucked it in and decided to go home. That would make her the most sensible of you all."

"Elizabeth has a head on her shoulders, I'll grant you that," Maggie said, "but she wouldn't leave us without saying anything."

"Why not?"

"Sh-she's gone, Mr. Slocum," Rachel got out. "We know she's been kidnapped. Elizabeth would never just up and leave without telling us."

"Why not?" Slocum repeated.

"She's the one who—" started Comfort, only to be silenced by a hot look from Maggie.

"Look, we got to move out, Slocum. Sell us the wagon and team. We want to get to Leadville."

"Without Elizabeth?" he asked. Maggie's reaction puzzled him. She seemed in a big hurry to get over the mountains, but having Elizabeth with her was important.

"We want her to come with us," Maggie said, chewing on her lower lip.

"You know how to drive a yoke of oxen?" Slocum asked. "No, I didn't think so," he said, seeing the expression on the women's faces. "What happened with Elizabeth? Tell me everything."

Slocum cursed himself because this was not his fight. The brunette had probably wandered off and gotten lost or perhaps she had decided the trip over the Front Range was too much for her and had sought a way home, wherever that might be. Elizabeth could have left without telling the others because she feared they would talk her into continuing.

Slocum snorted. Maggie looked to be the kind of dominating woman who could talk anyone into anything.

"We talked a spell after you left last night," Rachel said. "Elizabeth was upset over something but never owned up as to what it might be."

"That the last time you saw her?"

"I heard someone moving around outside the wagon a couple hours before sunup," said Comfort. "This place is like a train station. People come and go all the time, so I didn't think much about it."

"Now what do you think?" asked Slocum.

"Elizabeth wasn't in her bed. It was dark. Maggie had turned down the lantern and shadows can be confusing, but I don't think she was in the wagon."

Slocum considered how hard it might be to find the wayward woman. Or had Elizabeth been kidnapped, as Maggie thought? Something in the way the redhead spoke told Slocum he had not been told everything. Maggie didn't strike him as the kind to make up wild stories or play "what-if" games. She thought it more likely that Elizabeth had been kidnapped rather than simply wandered off.

"Will you find her, Mr. Slocum?" asked Comfort. The blonde put her warm hand on his arm and squeezed gently. "I could make it well worth your time. We don't have much money, but I'm sure we can figure out some other reward . . ."

Her bright blue eyes held worlds of promise. Slocum was not sure he need even find Elizabeth to collect on the promised reward the woman offered so eagerly. He looked at the other two women. Rachel was withdrawn and Maggie glared at him—or was it at Comfort for her blatant offering of sexual favors? Slocum could not tell.

"Where's she from?" he asked.

"Who? Oh, Elizabeth," said Maggie, getting back to the matter at hand. "She's from Kansas City, same as us. She would never go back there on her own."

"Who would want to kidnap her?" asked Slocum, not sure where to begin hunting for a woman amid all these pilgrims heading out to find their fortunes. If the women's intent was to find rich husbands, perhaps Elizabeth had the jump on the other three and had found one here in Denver.

Maggie and Rachel exchanged glances, then the red-haired woman shook her head. "Can't say."

Slocum damned himself for being doubly a fool, going off on what was likely to be a wild-goose chase without finding out the truth from these women. Maggie obviously held back details that would help him.

He could walk away and find someone to buy the wagon and team, then ride off and never look back. But the notion that Elizabeth had been kidnapped would ride with him and fester in him like a deeply buried thorn.

"I'll be back when I find her," Slocum said. As he turned, Comfort grabbed him and kissed him full on the lips. She looked up at him, her blue eyes glowing.

"Hurry back for your reward," she said in a husky whisper. Maggie grabbed the blonde's arm and pulled her back.

Slocum didn't know whether to thank Maggie or spend the rest of the day with Comfort. But he knew his conscience would nag him until he found out what had happened to Elizabeth. Slocum mounted his horse and rode slowly through the camp, trying to spot the brunette from his mount. He rode aimlessly for almost twenty minutes, then settled down into asking questions and trying to find the truth of the matter.

Another hour passed, and Slocum succeeded in finding out enough hard evidence to really tear at his gut. The women had been right about Elizabeth not going off on her own. More than one pilgrim had mentioned seeing Elizabeth with a man. Some said he shoved her along. Others said she went willingly enough. One had seen Elizabeth close enough to say he envied the man with her, giving a good description of the woman but not of the man.

Slocum got to the edge of the Auraria field and looked

across Cherry Creek toward Denver. The sluggishly flow-
ing stream mostly iced over during the night, but the
warm autumn sun broke tiny floes free to twist about and
shine like diamonds in the morning light. Slocum looked
to the far bank and saw where someone had made their
way up. He crossed the stream and examined the tracks.
He had no idea what kind of shoes Elizabeth wore, but a
man in boots had accompanied a woman with a narrow
foot up the muddy slopes.

Slocum felt a rush of confidence that he was on the
right trail. The two who had gone up the slope had crossed
the stream from the Auraria side. The chance of two others—other than Elizabeth and her kidnapper—making
those tracks was slim. At the top of the bank, Slocum
looked around and hardly believed his eyes.

Not a hundred feet away, Larson harangued someone
hidden from Slocum's sight by a canvas lean-to. The
tracks he followed led in that direction. Slocum made sure
his Colt Navy slid easily in his holster, then rode slowly
toward Larson.

The man heard Slocum's approach and spun about,
hand flying to his six-shooter. Slocum was faster and more
accurate with his shot. The Colt Navy barked and Larson
stumbled back, a round hitting him in the thigh. Slocum
saw a tiny cloud of blood flying from the wound, then the
man crashed flat on his back to the ground.

"Try to lift that hogleg and I'll kill you," Slocum told
Larson. The wounded man looked like a trapped rat. Slocum knew how dangerous a man in that condition was,
so he had to do something to let Larson know he was not
kidding. He aimed his Colt Navy and cocked it. The man
on the ground had to be looking straight down the barrel.
The Colt was only .36 caliber, but Slocum knew that any
six-gun looked like a fire hose when you were staring at
its business end.

"John? Is that you?" came a tiny voice.

"Elizabeth!" called Slocum. "Are you tied up?"

"I—"

Slocum's attention wavered for a moment when the canvas tent flapped and the woman tried to pull herself up and around. This gave Larson the chance he needed to roll out from under Slocum's muzzle and get his feet under him. The man dug his toes into the muddy ground, and he lit out like someone had set fire to his tail.

Slocum lifted his six-shooter and started to shoot at Larson. It was not a hard shot, but Slocum was no back-shooter. He left things like that to Larson and his ilk. Lowering his Colt Navy, he dismounted and went to see to Elizabeth.

The woman had been hobbled like a horse. Slocum stared at the tangle of rope for a moment, then slid it off her feet. He couldn't help noticing how slim and sleek her leg was. Elizabeth chastely pushed her skirt down.

"You hurt?" he asked. The woman shook her head. Except for the loose loops of rope around her ankles, she had not been tied up.

"I don't know how to thank you, John. You saved me."

"Why'd Larson kidnap you?" he asked point-blank. Her eyebrows shot up.

"You know him?"

"I ran into him last night." Slocum frowned as he considered Larson and how their paths had crossed. He had filled the man with more lead than he usually spent, and had the feeling Larson might have been the killer he had winged after Voss was shot.

"He's an awful man," Elizabeth said, shuddering and putting her arms around herself as if she were cold.

"How do you know him?"

"We . . . I knew him back home."

"Where's that?" Slocum asked, fishing for information to help him straighten out the tangle.

"St. Louis," she said quickly. "Yes, St. Louis. He was

sweet on me, but I didn't care for him and told him so. He followed me out here."

"You threw in with Maggie and the others and he still tracked you halfway across the country?"

"Yes," she said. "He's a terrible man. Not like you. You saved me. You risked your life. I am sure Larson is . . . is a killer. There's nothing about him that appeals to me." She turned brown eyes up to Slocum, and he wondered anew what he had gotten himself into.

She reached out and laid her hand on his arm, gently pulling him down to sit beside her.

"I'm cold, John. Warm me."

A dozen questions boiled up inside Slocum, all needing answers before he could go on. But Elizabeth's soft, wet lips closed on his and stifled any questions. He remembered Comfort's offer and then forgot it. Elizabeth was the one of the four he found most enticing—and she was obviously also as willing as Comfort to reward him for his bravery.

Her tongue slipped from between her ruby lips and danced lightly over his. She turned and crushed her breasts hard against his chest. Her weight forced him down onto the ground, the thin pallet under him and the lean-to flapping fitfully above.

"Someone might see us," he said. They were on the edge of Denver, after all, and the sun had been up for a couple hours. People went about their business.

"Don't worry about that, Larson chose this place because no one comes over here much from town." Elizabeth applied her mouth to his again and Slocum began forgetting everything but how much he desired her.

The woman's clever hand unfastened his gun belt and then popped open his buttoned fly, letting his manhood slip free. She caught it up and stroked slowly, warmly, getting it rigid. When Slocum grunted at how much it was beginning to pain him, Elizabeth pulled back a mite and grinned at him.

"Don't worry," she said. "Don't worry about anything."

Slocum started to reply, but the woman swung her leg over his supine body. She wiggled her hips and settled her skirts and then he felt the warmth of her most intimate recess brush across the tip of his shaft. Elizabeth obviously did not bother with the frilly undergarments so many women wore.

She moved her hips a bit more, and Slocum sank into paradise. Warm, clutching female flesh surrounded him. Elizabeth got her knees up on either side of his body and began rocking back and forth, taking him fully into her moist center and then slowly moving away. All their lovemaking was hidden under her billowy skirts.

Slocum lay back and let the woman move; her actions were fully satisfying. He craned his neck a mite so he could kiss her on the lips. His hands roamed over her back and then around to cup her breasts, still hidden under her blouse. Through the cotton he felt her hot nipples pulse with desire and stiffen to points like accusing fingers. He rolled them around, pressing hard until Elizabeth gasped with pleasure.

"So nice, John, so nice. And you fill me so!"

She began rotating her hips, moving in bigger and bigger circles until he thought she would tear his manhood from his groin. She rocked back and grabbed his hands, forcing them down hard on her breasts as she tossed her head back like a frisky filly. Rising and falling, she twisted with every movement until the heat of friction filled Slocum's loins.

Elizabeth gasped and moaned and began slamming her hips down forcefully before grinding them into Slocum's groin. He felt her ecstasy before the gasp of ultimate pleasure escaped her lips. All around him she tensed and assaulted him with her inner heat.

Moaning, sobbing, thrashing about, she rose and fell on his fleshy column until Slocum was no longer able to hold back. His balls tightened, and he exploded like a stick of dynamite hidden away in a mine shaft. The eruption caused the woman to shudder and writhe about with even more intensity. Then, as he turned limp, she sagged forward and lay with her cheek against his. Elizabeth's warm breath gusted past his ear and she murmured, "Thank you, John. Thank you so much."

"I'm the one who ought to be thanking you," he said. "I never expected this."

"You deserve it for saving me from . . . from him." Elizabeth could not bring herself to even say Larson's name.

"He's gone, run off. He won't be back." Slocum sighed, knowing they could not lie like this the rest of the day. Gently dislodging her, he sat up and worked to get his jeans buttoned and his gun belt fastened. Elizabeth smoothed down her skirts. Except for the flush remaining on her neck and shoulders, he would never have guessed what she had been up to.

"What now?" she asked.

"We get back to the wagon. Then the five of us need to decide what's going to happen next."

"You won't take us to Leadville, will you? Now that Voss is dead, I don't know what we're going to do."

"Go home to Kansas City," he said. She jumped. "Or St. Louis. Wherever it's more civilized. You don't belong out on the frontier."

"You can't know," Elizabeth muttered. Louder, she said, "Please, John. It won't be that difficult for you. Take us to Leadville."

"Come on," he said, standing. He offered Elizabeth his hand and helped her up. He noticed she moved a little slow. Their lovemaking had taken its toll on her, too. He almost dragged her along to where his horse stood patiently. Slocum helped Elizabeth into the saddle, then mounted behind her.

"We can pay, John. We don't have much money because we'd already given so much to Voss, but we can get more."

"By marrying rich miners?" he scoffed. "I've got all the money I need, thank you." The horse edged down the muddy slope and back across Cherry Creek into Auraria. Slocum found the going a little harder because so many of the wagons had left, robbing him of markers back to the wagon where he had left Maggie and the other two.

"Where are we going, John?" Elizabeth asked after they had ridden around for a half hour.

"I don't rightly know. I thought the wagon was parked about here, but I don't see it anywhere."

Slocum went cold inside when he saw deep ruts leading west, toward the Front Range. Maggie and the others had taken off on their own. In his wagon.

4

"They're gone," Elizabeth said in a voice almost too low for Slocum to hear. He had expected some fear on her part, some other reaction than the one he got. Had the other women been kidnapped, also? But he heard more anger than anxiety.

"They can't get too far. Do any of them know how to drive a wagon?" he asked. Slocum read the answer on the woman's lovely face, now twisted into something approaching real ire that the other three women had upped and left her behind.

"I doubt it," Elizabeth said. "That's why we needed Voss. Or you, John. We need you to help us get to Leadville." She twisted even more in the saddle in front of him, trying to face him squarely. Her leg pressed warmly into his, but Slocum would not be distracted.

"They lit out in *my* wagon," Slocum reminded her. "They stole what belongs to me. I hadn't decided what to do with the wagon and team, but going over Mosquito Pass this close to the edge of winter wasn't what I intended."

"Please," the woman pleaded. "Let's find them, then we can talk this out. It's so important to us. To me. I'm really grateful for all you've done for me so far. I can be even more appreciative if you help us get to Leadville."

Slocum took a deep breath to settle his nerves. He felt jumpier than ever listening to Elizabeth's entreaty. What the women said and what they wanted in Leadville were two different things. He knew it. No woman risked what these four already had just to marry a grimy miner, no matter how big his stash.

Turning his horse's face in the direction of the looming mountains, Slocum started riding, his eyes on the deep ruts left by the wagon. By *his* wagon.

His arms around the woman's supple waist felt mighty good, and Elizabeth had shown she was willing to thank him delightfully for whatever services he might provide. But Slocum knew he was being used and did not like it one iota. When he found the wagon and its cargo, he ought to either throw them out beside the road and sell the entire rig to the first man with two coins to rub together or just give them the Conestoga along with his good wishes for a safe journey.

He ought to do one or the other. Deep down, Slocum worried he wouldn't show that much good sense.

Twenty minutes later, he spotted the lumbering Conestoga on a narrow road heading north off the main course. By this time his own anger at the three women boiled over. Slocum put his heels to the pony's flanks and picked up the pace to overtake the wagon. He wanted this over and done with.

Sitting in the back, her long legs dangling over the edge, sat Comfort. The blonde waved and smiled prettily.

"Yoo-hoo, Mr. Slocum, hello!" she called.

"Pull over," Slocum shouted.

"John, don't be too hard on them," spoke up Elizabeth. "They just did what they thought was right."

"Letting a kidnapper keep you, stealing my wagon and team, those are the right things to do?" Slocum swallowed some of his anger when he saw Rachel moving through the wagon. The dark-haired woman looked frightened, but then she always seemed ready to turn and run.

"Maggie," called Comfort. "Mr. Slocum's got Elizabeth with him. We're all together again."

The road turned slightly, giving him a view of the red-haired woman struggling with the oxen. To him it looked as if Maggie tried to whip the team into giving more speed. That showed what she knew about oxen. They had one speed and kept to it, no matter the terrain. Uphill or down, oxen pulled at their own rate and no one, even expert mule skinners, got more from them.

"Pull over," Slocum called when he got even with the driver's box. Maggie lifted the whip, as if she might try using it on him, then sagged. She secured the whip in its holder, then put her feet hard against the front of the box, tugging on the reins to slow and then stop the oxen. The wagon lurched and then tilted to one side, as if she had driven off the road into a ditch.

"I'm glad to see you three again," Elizabeth said, an edge in her voice.

"We're happy you're safe," Maggie said, equally cold. She tried to stand in the uneven wagon and almost fell. Maggie grabbed hold of the edge of the wagon and pulled herself out to the ground, standing so she could glare at Elizabeth and Slocum.

Slocum wondered at the verbal tug-of-war between the women. It was as if Elizabeth challenged Maggie for leadership of this strange Amazonian band, and the only way Maggie hoped to win was to run off without the brunette. None of it made a bit of sense to him.

"Down you go," he said, putting his strong arm around Elizabeth's waist as he swept her from the saddle and lightly lowered her to the ground beside the wagon's front wheel.

"John, I owe you so much, saving me from Larson the

way you did," Elizabeth started. Slocum had the feeling she was speaking for the other women's benefit, to let them know what had happened.

"You owe me nothing, unless you want to buy the wagon and team."

"See us over the pass. You weren't heading anywhere in particular. I can tell. Help us."

"And you'll make it worth my while once you marry rich miners?" he finished sarcastically.

"Well, Mr. Slocum, it might just be worth your time *until* we do," spoke up coquettish Comfort. The blonde batted her long eyelashes and smiled at him.

"You hush up now, you hear?" snapped Maggie. "We can get along just fine without him, especially now that Elizabeth's back."

Again Slocum heard the challenge in the redhead's voice, reminding him of the way one bull elk trumpeted and called out another during rutting season for the right to rule the herd.

"You think you can get along without a guide?" Slocum asked, a smile creeping across his lips. He looked at the wagon and the road Maggie had found for it to cut deep tracks in.

"What's so funny?" she said testily.

"Where were you heading? Laramie, was it?"

"Spit it out, Slocum, say what you mean," Maggie said, her lips a thin line.

"You'll reach Wyoming before Leadville if you keep on this road. See over there? The big, tall mountains? Those are the Front Range, the ones you have to cross to get to Leadville. This road leads north into Wyoming."

"I thought the going was mighty easy," Rachel said, biting down on a knuckle and looking even more worried. "He's right, Maggie. The big mountains are over yonder."

"You'd find mountains if you kept on this road," Slocum said. He had come this way from the north when he had drifted into Denver. "In a week or so of travelling, that is."

"We need him, Maggie, we do," Elizabeth said, heading off the fiery redhead's angry retort. "You don't know how to drive the team. None of us do, and it's important to get to Leadville before it snows."

"I've said my piece on this before," Slocum said. "Wait until the spring thaw before you go. Being down here, out on the plains where it's warmer, can deceive you into thinking it'll be this way all the way over the pass. A sudden storm and you might end up frozen stiffer than one of the marble statues in front of the territorial governor's house."

"Oh, my, a man who is frozen stiff," mused Comfort, deep in mock thought. "Whatever would I do with such a man?"

"Be quiet, Comfort," said Maggie. She took a deep breath. Slocum couldn't help noticing the way her blouse lifted and then fell with just a hint of a jiggle. "Very well. Please accompany us, Mr. Slocum. We need help. We're nothing but helpless women and throw ourselves on your mercy."

"That's not where I want to throw myself," said Comfort. "From the look of it, that's not where Elizabeth wants to, either."

"Comfort, shut up!" bellowed Maggie.

The blonde was unfazed by the way Maggie shouted at her. She grinned and then slowly, sensually licked her lips for Slocum's benefit. He felt a mite uncomfortable with Elizabeth so close. Slocum did not owe her anything and had not expected her to reward him the way she had when he rescued her from Larson. But because she had, this shouldn't put any shackles around him, holding him to what might prove to be a suicidal trip into the mountains.

"We do need your help, Mr. Slocum. Please," said Rachel, coming up from the rear of the wagon.

Slocum did not reply. He looked at the road behind the wagon and in front, wondering why it canted so precipitously to the right. Riding around the wagon revealed the answer. The right front wheel nut had come undone when Maggie had slowed the oxen and now slanted off at a crazy angle. If he tried to drive off the wagon in this condition, he might break the axle.

For two cents, Slocum would have left the lot of them here on the prairie with the busted wagon.

If he'd had enough sense, he would never have gotten involved in the first place.

Slocum dismounted and pushed back his hat, studying the problem.

"What's wrong with it?" asked Rachel, coming up close. She brushed against him, just a hint of her breast touching his arm before she backed off as if he had burned her.

"Needs fixing," Slocum said laconically.

"If we help, will you drive us over the mountains?" asked Elizabeth.

"Voss must have had a wrench or other tools in the wagon. Get them," he said. Slocum tossed his hat to the ground and then fished out a pair of leather gloves from his saddlebags. He went to the wagon and turned away from it. He got his fingers curled under the wagon bed, widened his stance just enough and then waited for Elizabeth to return with the wrench.

"When I lift, get the wheel pushed back into place and then tighten that nut as fast as you can."

"You're going to lift the wagon all by yourself?" Elizabeth asked, her brown eyes wide in surprise. "Can you do it all alone?"

"If the other three want to help, I wouldn't complain," he said, but Slocum knew he was going to be the one doing the real work. "Get as much gear out of the wagon as you can, then we'll see if I've got what it takes."

"Oh, you do, you do," cooed Comfort. She pouted prettily when Maggie glared at her, then the women disappeared into the wagon, leaving Slocum to stew in his own juices. He was getting roped into doing something he knew was foolish and dangerous. Slocum muttered, "Get this wagon to the next town along the road, then that's it."

"What, John?" asked Elizabeth, returning with the big wrench.

"Everything out of the wagon?" he asked. The brunette nodded. Slocum took a deep breath, then began lifting. At first, the wood groaned as the weight came off it. Then Slocum realized his joints were making almost as much noise as the protesting wood and the nut turning sluggishly at the end of the axle.

"Hurry up," he grated out. Elizabeth hurried. She stepped back just as Slocum's strength fled. The wagon dropped to the ground. Slocum eyed the wheel and knew the nut was still loose. He needed a wheelwright to finish the chore. Returning to the field in Auraria was out of the question. Better to press on to the small town about a mile farther down the road.

"I've never seen a man so strong," Elizabeth said in a hushed voice. She took a step toward him, her hand reaching out to touch him, then froze when Maggie bustled around the wagon.

"Fixed? Let's settle accounts and—"

"The wagon needs expert repair. The wheel wouldn't get you ten miles before it came loose again," Slocum said, cutting her off. He pointed to the town ahead. "There. Head on for the town and we'll see to fixing the wheel."

He rode behind the wagon. Maggie and Elizabeth sat in the driver's box. The best he could tell, they argued constantly. Rachel huddled in the rear of the wagon, furtively looking in his direction, as if he might snap at her.

Comfort rode in her original position, legs draped over
the rear of the wagon, her bright blue eyes fixed on him.

He did not need to be a mind reader to know what
thoughts ran through the blonde's mind. Whatever miner
she married would be a dead man in a month. But dying
from the pleasurable exhaustion the blonde offered might
be worth it.

Slocum wasn't sure he wanted to find out, though.

"Crack runs the length of the axle. You try takin' this
wagon into Mosquito Pass and you'll be stuck within a
day," the wheelwright declared. "No way of fixin' it up
there in the mountains, either."

"What if you put on a new axle?" Slocum asked.

"Might work, but the wagon's heavy, too heavy for the
road across the mountains. You need a lighter, smaller
wagon, you and them ladies." The wheelwright chewed
on his lower lip as he watched the four women holding
court at the general store. Men flocked from all over town
to talk to them.

Slocum was not surprised when Comfort went off with
a well-dressed man, possibly a gambler or maybe the
owner of the town's only saloon. What did surprise him
was how Rachel took up readily with a farm boy hardly
dry behind the ears. Maggie and Elizabeth held back, but
not for long after Elizabeth came over and learned the
wagon couldn't be fixed any time soon.

"We're dickerin', little lady," the wheelwright said.
"Might be I can make you a good deal on a different
wagon, one better suited for travelin' where you want to
go."

"And how do you know where I want to go?" cooed
Elizabeth, her voice silky and seductive. It was as if Slocum wasn't even there.

"Reckon I have a good idea. Might be wrong, so's why
don't you tell me."

"Over dinner? After?" Elizabeth suggested. She and the wheelwright went off side by side, leaving Slocum with the wagon and team. He saw Maggie and a man dressed like a banker deep in intimate conversation. They trailed after Elizabeth and her new beau, heading for the town's only restaurant.

"If that doesn't beat all," Slocum said, shaking his head.

He knew he ought to leave the wagon and the women and hightail it. But his curiosity was getting the better of him. Why *did* they want to get to Leadville? It was a dangerous question to answer, but Slocum knew he was likely to stick around to find out.

He didn't have anywhere else to go, and the four women were certainly easy on the eyes. Even if the trip across the Front Range was likely to be anything but serene, Slocum reckoned he might find out what Leadville was like this time of year.

5

Slocum began to wonder if the wheelwright wanted them to ever leave the small town. The arrival of four such lovely women had to be the most excitement the sleepy town had seen in years. Slocum knew he ought to head out. The wheelwright or someone else might be willing to buy the wagon. Still, the notion of duty came to Slocum. He had promised to swap the heavier Conestoga for a lighter wagon able to traverse the narrow pass over the Front Range.

Lying back in the straw-stacked stall with his hands folded under his head, Slocum stared at the stable roof and thought hard on his predicament. He owed the women nothing. If anything, they were beholden to him. He had rescued Elizabeth from a kidnapper. As that thought came, another, more disturbing one, replaced it. Larson seemed the kind to murder Voss, but something about Elizabeth and Larson together struck Slocum as wrong. Had he really kidnapped her or had she gone with him willingly, then changed her mind?

There had been no mistaking how thankful she was for Slocum rescuing her.

And he had pulled Maggie and the other two women's

fat out of the fire when the wagon wheel broke down. They might still be on the wrong road with a busted wagon if he had not saved them. He seemed to be the only one doing any rescuing of such beautiful women.

Slocum snorted and wondered if he could ever think of them as ladies after the way they had cut out men from the crowd and corralled them so quickly. He had never seen a soiled dove in a dance hall work faster or better. They had sniffed out the men with money and were off with them now like any whore he had ever seen. Still, he had a hard time thinking of them as whores, even if that seemed to be the way they acted.

Truth was, he could not figure out how he thought of them. They were such a mismatched group but with a single-minded determination to reach Leadville. That, as much as anything else, intrigued him and would probably get him into a whale of a lot of trouble. Though he only vaguely realized that he had come to a decision, he knew he was going to swap for the smaller wagon and see them to the end of the trail.

He sat up, his hand going to his six-gun when he heard the barn door creaking open. A shadowy figure slipped into the stable, then tugged the door closed.

Slocum waited, not sure what was going on. Then he saw Comfort pass by the stall where he had spread his bedroll for the night.

"Evening," he said. The blond woman jumped as if he had stuck her with a pin. She turned and faced him, her hand at her throat.

Comfort had to be a better actress than he gave her credit for to put on such a frightened face.

"You scared me, John. I was looking for you but didn't think you were here. I mean, I knew you were here, but not *here*, if you know what I mean."

He had never seen her this flustered.

"What's wrong?" he asked, getting up and brushing

straw off himself. She stepped forward hesitantly. He had expected a bolder move on her part after all the brazen words Comfort had sent his way since they had first met.

"I—" She swallowed hard and looked away. Then she fixed her blue eyes on his green ones and said, "It's this town. I don't like it, John. I need to hide out."

"Hide from what?" he asked. He expected her to move closer and make a play for him, but again she surprised him. She seemed to close in on herself.

"Can I trust you?" Comfort spun about, then turned more slowly to face him. "What am I saying? Of course I can trust you. That's why I came here. You helped Elizabeth and the rest of us when you didn't have to, so of course I can trust you." She took a deep breath, her ample bosom rising and falling. This time Slocum didn't think there was any guile to her actions. She wasn't pushing herself at him as much as collecting her thoughts.

He stayed silent, knowing that sooner or later she would fill the void with an explanation. To his surprise, he found himself wanting to hear it. This might be a key to finding out more about the four women.

"The town marshal," she blurted. "I'm afraid he might know me."

"So?" Slocum had wanted posters on him floating around the West. Right after the war he had returned to Calhoun, Georgia, and Slocum's Stand, which had been in the Slocum family since the days of George II. He had returned to an abandoned farm, his parents and brother dead. All Slocum had wanted to do was recuperate from a vicious belly wound and to live peacefully. A carpetbagger judge had other ideas, saying the taxes had been neglected.

When the judge and a hired gunman had ridden out to seize the farm, they had found more than they bargained for. At the end of the day, Slocum had turned his back on two new graves and headed west. For the killing of a

Yankee judge, he had a warrant put on his head he could never outrun. And if killing a judge had been all, he might not have worried as much about some backwater marshal seeing his picture on a wanted poster.

His life had been less than pure, and his quarrels more often than not deadly.

What had Comfort gotten herself mixed up in?

"I don't know how to say this, John, so I'll just come right out and tell you. I shot a man. Back in Kansas City. He was awful to me and I took his gun and I shot him! I'm not proud of it, but he hurt me bad. It was the only way I could get away from him."

"Seems you and Elizabeth have that much in common," Slocum said. Comfort's eyes widened in surprise.

"What do you mean, John?"

"She came out West to get away from Larson. Funny she never mentioned that to you." This was a shot in the dark, but one which explained much of what he had seen.

"Larson? The man who took her?" Comfort mulled this over, as if it were all new territory for her. "I didn't know."

For the women to have traveled all the way from the Mississippi River to the middle of Colorado Territory they had spent damned little time telling each other about their pasts. From all Slocum had seen of women, this seemed unusual.

Then again, everything about the four women was unusual.

"You hiding out?" he asked. "Is the marshal hunting you down?"

"I don't think so, but he was eyeing me strangely. I might be running when there's no reason, but he looked at me like he was trying to remember where he had seen me before. Not a lusting look, but one of business. Law business."

"You figure he's trailing you?"

The blonde nodded. Any coquetry that had been in her had long since vanished. Slocum believed her when she told him how worried she was that the marshal might remember where he had put a wanted poster on her.

"You kill him? The man in Kansas City? Or did you just wound him?"

Comfort shook her head. "I must have killed him. I didn't stay around to find out."

Slocum wondered if it was only guilty conscience plaguing the pretty blonde or if there really was a wanted poster on her. Whichever it was, she told the truth. She had gunned down a man and had spent too much time listening for the footsteps of a lawman behind her.

"I'll see what I can do," Slocum said. "You're safe enough here. If anyone comes in, just burrow under the straw and hide."

"What are you going to do, John? If you kill a lawman, they'll swarm all over us and we'll never get away."

"I don't shoot someone unless there's a reason," he said. "Might be you remind him of a lost wife. The marshal might have a perfectly innocent reason for looking like he did at you. I can poke around in his office and see if he's got a wanted poster with your picture on it."

"If he does?" Comfort asked apprehensively.

"Reckon I'd steal it so I'll have a picture to remember you by when they send you to jail," Slocum said, grinning at her. Comfort straightened in outrage, then relaxed when she realized he was only joshing her.

"Thank you," she said simply. Again she surprised him. She made no move to kiss him when it would have been a perfectly reasonable way of sending him on his way.

Slocum settled his gun at his left hip and then stepped into the cold night air. The clouds had lifted, leaving the stars shining down brightly and lighting the way as good as any gaslight in Denver might have. The lone saloon in town was the logical place to start. If Slocum placed the marshal there, he could look through the wanted posters in the lawman's office without being disturbed.

He poked his head through the swinging doors, then jerked back suddenly, his heart pounding. Slocum had wanted to find the marshal. Instead of a hick town lawman he had found trouble. Big trouble.

A mountain of a man knocked back shots of cheap whiskey at the bar, hardly noticing the sharp bite or the kick of the alcohol when it reached his bulging belly. The smell of bear grease wafted from the direction of the mountain of gristle and mean, and Slocum knew Bear Zacharias was on his trail.

Slocum had had three run-ins with Zacharias over the past year. The bounty hunter had found one of those wanted posters with a two-hundred dollar reward for judge killing and had thought bringing Slocum in beat working for a living. Twice they had shot it out, each of them taking a bullet from the other's six-gun. The third time Slocum had thought he had killed the bounty hunter, leaving him at the bottom of a canyon after he and Zacharias had duked it out on the edge of a cliff. Slocum had connected with the man's protruding belly and had knocked him over the rim. He had been in too much of a hurry to see if the fall had actually killed Zacharias.

Slocum had hoped it had. But he had been wrong. Either that or Bear Zacharias had a twin brother. That was more of a coincidence than Slocum wanted to believe.

Moving to the side of the saloon, Slocum edged closer to a window where he might get a better look. Bear Zacharias stood with his back to the window, giving Slocum only a few more details. But he knew this had to be the bounty hunter he had thought was dead. Two men couldn't be this big, this ugly and smell this bad.

Slocum slipped his Colt Navy from its holster. He wasn't much for shooting a man in the back, but for Zacharias he would make an exception. He lifted his six-shooter and then hesitated when he heard the bounty hunter's gruff question of the barkeep.

"Them wimmen. The purty ones. How long they been in town?"

"Just blew in today," the barkeep said. "You want another, uh, bottle?"

"Yeah, gimme," said Zacharias. His ham of a hand curled around the new whiskey bottle, engulfing it. This time he didn't bother with a glass but downed a hefty slug straight from the bottle. Zacharias belched, then put the bottle on the bar. "The gold-haired one. What do you know of her?"

The barkeep shrugged, indicating he knew nothing. Zacharias wasn't going to take this as an answer. He reached for the barkeep when a wisp of a woman fluttered up. To Slocum's surprise, Rachel put her hand on Zacharias's and kept him from throttling the bartender.

"You're asking after a friend of mine," the timid dark-haired woman said. But there was no quaver in her voice as she looked directly up into the bounty hunter's face.

"Am I now, you sweet li'l thang?" Zacharias said.

"What do you want with her when you can talk to me?" Rachel moved a little closer to the bounty hunter and ran her fingers up and down the front of his greasy buckskins. "My, you are a big one. I like that."

Slocum hardly believed his ears. Rachel had taken up right away with a farm boy. That had made sense. The sodbuster probably was as shy as Rachel. Or how he thought Rachel was. Slocum realized these four women constantly startled him with the way they changed like a mirage in the desert. Just when he thought he had a handle on them, they turned into something entirely different.

"I'm lookin' fer a woman. Comfort's her name."

"Look no farther if it's comfort you want," Rachel said, sidling even closer and rubbing against the bounty hunter as if she were a cat greeting her master. "Or would you rather get some . . . relief?"

"There's a matter of a reward."

"I'll show you rewards," Rachel promised.

Slocum lifted his six-shooter again, then shoved it hard into his holster. Rachel and Zacharias wandered off, heading toward the rear of the saloon to do who knows what. Slocum didn't want to dwell too long on the possibilities. The women had seemed like sex-starved whores when they saw the crowd around them. What more were they?

His head hurting at the possibilities, Slocum backed from the window and then quickly returned to the livery.

"Comfort?" he called softly. "You still here?"

"Yes, John, under the pile of straw." He saw the fresh straw waiting to be pitched into the stalls move. A ghostly figure rose from under it and took form. Comfort.

"I've got a question to ask," he said.

"What is it?" Comfort could have taken the opportunity to cling to his arm and rub herself against his body as Rachel had done with Zacharias. She remained aloof, as if her fright was growing.

"You know a bounty hunter named Bear Zacharias?"

"I don't think so," she said, obviously thinking hard on the matter. "Should I?"

"You'll have to ask Rachel," Slocum answered.

"I don't understand."

"Get your belongings together. I've got to get you out of town fast."

"Then leave my luggage," Comfort said. "It won't be the first time I had to travel with only the clothing on my back."

Slocum was curious but did not ask for details. He grabbed a couple of blankets and some grub from a box at the rear of the livery, then saddled his horse. He mounted and let Comfort ride behind him, figuring she could hide her face better this way.

Slowly riding from town, he angled away from the road and struck out in a beeline for the main trail leading into Mosquito Pass. The cold wind whipped down from the higher elevations and cut at his face, making him wish he had a scarf. His body blocked the worst of the wind from Comfort. The blonde clung to him but made no play for him, as he half expected.

For an hour they rode, then he spotted a gully protected from the fierce wind. Urging his horse down, he found a pocket shielded by the tall banks of an arroyo. He gathered wood and started a fire for the woman.

Comfort warmed her hands by the guttering campfire, her shoulders hunched over. She looked utterly miserable. Slocum felt a pang of guilt about leaving her, but he saw no way around it.

"You've got blankets enough to keep you warm. There's plenty of wood, and here's some food for breakfast."

"You'll be back?" she asked in a little-girl-lost voice.

"With the wagon and your friends," Slocum said. Any notion he had once entertained about leaving the four of them to cross the pass on their own vanished. He had come up against Bear Zacharias and knew how implacable the man was when he scented a reward. If he caught Comfort, she was a goner.

No matter what had happened in Kansas City, whether she had defended herself as she said or murdered the man in cold blood, she did not deserve to be taken into custody by the bounty hunter. That was about the same as a death sentence.

"Thank you, John," Comfort said. She smiled weakly, and Slocum knew he could never abandon her.

The ride back to town seemed like a thousand miles.

6

Slocum rode back into the small town, more tired than he could remember being in a dozen years. Doing the right thing by the women was proving to be exhausting. Still, he could not abandon them to the likes of Bear Zacharias. Whatever the bounty hunter wanted with Comfort could not be good. Whatever Zacharias wanted with *anybody* could not be good.

For two cents Slocum would plug the son of a bitch.

Slocum remembered his chance at backshooting the bounty hunter as he drank in the saloon and almost regretted not taking the shot. He was no dry-gulcher, not by nature, but it would have saved him a whale of a lot of trouble. Even as he considered what it had felt like, his trigger finger tightening as he sighted in on the bounty hunter's broad back, another thought rose to bother him.

Rachel. She had acted strangely for a woman trying to protect a friend from the bounty hunter. Slocum could not figure her out at all. She acted mousy and meek, then turned into a real man-eater as soon as she got out among men in a small town. Worse, she put Zacharias in her sights and, if Slocum had to guess, hit a bull's-eye with him. Why? For that Slocum had no answer.

He dismounted at the side of the livery stable and cautiously poked his head inside, worrying just a little that Zacharias might have laid a trap for them. Instead, he saw the wheelwright working on a set of spokes, shaping one and then laying it at his feet to start another.

The man looked up and said, "Come on in. I think I got a wagon lined up for you, if you want to make the swap."

"That I do," Slocum said. He entered the stable, still wary of Zacharias jumping out to grab him. Slocum relaxed as he took a few steps and saw he and the wheelwright were alone. He had to discount his jumpiness as being too long in the saddle and—as much as he hated to admit it—spooked by the bounty hunter's presence. Slocum had thought Zacharias was a broken, dead man at the bottom of a cliff. Seeing him again was bad enough. Finding that he was on Comfort's trail drove yet another nail into the coffin.

"Even-steven," the wheelwright said, wiping his hands on his thighs. "The Conestoga for something a bit larger than a buckboard." He saw the expression on Slocum's face and hurriedly added, "But big enough for you and the ladies and all your supplies. And a team of four mules. You don't want them oxen pullin' a light wagon over gravelly trails. You need surefooted mules."

"The wagon, the mules and enough supplies in trade for the Conestoga and yoke of oxen," Slocum countered.

"Can't do that. Wouldn't make any money. The axle's cracked and—"

Slocum and the wheelwright dickered for another five minutes until they shook on their deal. Although Slocum was not pleased with bartering away supplies, he got a good water barrel and two extra mules. Six strong mules pulling a light wagon would let them make better time through the pass.

The supplies the women already had would be a good

start, but Slocum wanted more. He had to see what the new wagon would take. Overloading it and having an axle break halfway through Mosquito Pass was a surefire way to die if a storm blew in on them.

Slocum and the wheelwright went outside and walked to the end of town where the new wagon stood. Looking it over showed Slocum that the wheelwright was an honest businessman. Everything he had said about the wagon was true. He was less satisfied with the condition of the six mules, but everyone exaggerated about animals, and Slocum saw nothing to jeopardize them using this team. He started shifting their supplies. As he worked, he wondered where he would find the three women.

Maggie and Elizabeth would be no problem. If Rachel was still with Zacharias, there would be nothing but bullets and blood. His worries did not pan out. Before he finished storing the women's trunks in the wagon bed, the three came hurrying up. Slocum glanced up and saw it was about an hour after sunrise.

"Mr. Slocum, my, you have been busy," Elizabeth greeted. She moved closer, ran her hand over his back and whispered, "I wish you had been around last night. We could have had *so* much fun!"

"Other things came up," Slocum said, fixing his gaze on Rachel. "I had to get Comfort out of town fast."

"Why?" gruffly demanded Maggie.

"A bounty hunter is after her. His name's Zacharias. Bear Zacharias. A big bruiser." Slocum watched Rachel's reaction, but he might have been talking about someone she had never seen in her young life. The more he saw of these women, the less he understood.

"She's safe?" Elizabeth asked anxiously.

"She's outside town a ways. Get in the wagon and let's drive. I want out of here as fast as we can go."

"Mules?" Maggie curled her lip, sneering at the new team.

"They're tastier than oxen, if we have to eat them," Slocum said. This shocked the redhead enough to get her moving. She climbed into the rear of the wagon with Rachel. Elizabeth was already in the driver's box, waiting for him. After the way she had headed into town to go whoring, Slocum was not sure he wanted anything to do with her. But like Rachel, she seemed to have forgotten she ever sidled up to any of the men. It was as if this Elizabeth was a different woman from the one he had seen the night before.

"You ever work as a mule skinner, John?" she asked when she saw how he expertly took the whip and snapped it just above the mules' long ears and got the animals pulling.

"Not many things I haven't tried, at least for a while," Slocum said. He cracked the whip again, this time barely nipping the lead mule. The beast jumped and began pulling with a vengeance. Slocum was glad to see such obliging mules. Some might have balked. With six working, they pulled the wagon and its load easily.

"I can believe that," Elizabeth said seductively. "Back in Denver, under that lean-to, we—"

"I don't want to talk about it. The pass is going to take all our energy, and I need to concentrate on getting us to Leadville alive."

Elizabeth frowned but said nothing. She turned, put her hands chastely in her lap and stared straight ahead. Her silence suited Slocum just fine. Slocum found himself arguing with himself about getting mixed up in these four women's misadventures. He knew nothing about them or why they were so het up about getting to Leadville. It wasn't to snare themselves rich husbands. Or was it? They certainly cut the best bulls out of the herd in the town that was now more than a mile behind them. He might have watched them practicing their wiles for when they found the right men.

The right *rich* men.

"Where'd you abandon Comfort?" called Maggie from the rear of the wagon. The canvas over the load flapped noisily as the wind blowing off the Front Range turned increasingly bitter. The redhead crawled forward, holding the canvas down with her hands and knees as she made her way forward.

"Didn't abandon her, left her where she'd be safe," Slocum said, irritated at the way Maggie twisted what he had done. "Would you rather I'd turned her over to Zacharias? You don't know how persistent that son of a bitch can be."

"All we have is your word that this so-called bounty hunter is after her."

"Ask Rachel," he said, turning so he could watch the road and tend the mules. Somehow, the act of driving shut out Maggie and Elizabeth and the troubles they carried with them. He heard Maggie settle down, then work her way to the rear of the wagon. Whether she asked Rachel mattered little to Slocum. He settled into the rhythm of driving and ignored everything else until around noon when he caught sight of the ravine where he had left Comfort the night before.

A thin spiral of wood smoke rose from the protected area. Rather than drive down into the sandy-bottomed arroyo, he pulled the mules to a halt, then jumped down.

"John, where are you going?" Elizabeth asked anxiously. "You're not leaving us out here, are you?"

"You worry too much," he said. This was something else he could not get a handle on. The women swung back and forth between total independence, devil take the hindmost, and acting afraid of being left behind. For two cents, he'd do that very thing, get on his horse and ride off.

Then he saw how miserable Comfort was, huddled under her saddle blankets by the sputtering fire. She had used most all the firewood he had collected, and he

doubted she had gone hunting for more. The blonde
looked up and her face lit up like a summer sunrise.

"John! You're back!"

"I got the others with me. We need to get on the road
to the pass. I want to be in the foothills before nightfall."

"Sundown comes faster the closer we get to the Front
Range," Comfort said. "Those are mighty tall mountains."

"Come along," he said, helping her to the wagon. Maggie and Rachel jumped down and threw their arms around
her. Elizabeth was slower to greet her friend. Slocum had
the feeling Elizabeth thought more had gone on between
him and the blonde than really had.

He climbed into the driver's box and waited for the
four to get into the wagon bed. Then Slocum got the
mules moving. The road through Mosquito Pass came on
him suddenly, but he welcomed the sight of the well-
traveled ruts going up into the foothills. He had been over
the pass several times and knew how quickly and steeply
the road rose into the heart of the mountains. It would not
be an easy trip.

The mules pulled faithfully, lulling Slocum into a
dreamy state that almost got him killed.

Stones rattled under the wagon wheels and occasionally
bounced off the underside of the wagon like tiny bullet
ricochets. Slocum had grown so used to the sound he
didn't recognize the real flight of a bullet past his head
until a second slug ripped off part of his hat brim.

Ducking, he swung around trying to locate the bushwhacker. He worried that Zacharias had found them, that
the bounty hunter had left town and positioned himself
along the road waiting for Comfort to try to escape to
Leadville. Then he knew how ridiculous that was. How
could Zacharias possibly know Comfort was headed to
Leadville?

Unless Rachel had told him.

Three new rounds forced Slocum to crouch down in

the driver's box for the little protection the thin wood sides afforded him. He looked around frantically but couldn't figure out where the hail of lead came from.

"Stay down!" he shouted when Maggie scampered forward to ask what was going on. "Stay down unless you want your head blown off!"

"What have you gotten us into, Slocum?" Maggie cried angrily.

He did not bother answering such a ridiculous charge.

Slocum's Winchester rode in the saddle sheath on his tethered horse, trotting along behind the wagon. He had his trusty Colt Navy, but from the reports now echoing along the rising canyon walls on either side of the road, their attacker was using a rifle. If the women had not been in the wagon, Slocum would have halted the mules and made a stand. But he dared not risk their lives and kept the mules pulling hard to get away from the ambush.

"Keep a sharp eye out," Slocum called to Maggie. "Find where the bushwhacker is hiding."

"Can't see a thing, Slocum."

He drove around a bend in the road, the steep canyon walls cutting off any attack from behind. The sun had set behind the mountains. Comfort had been all too right about how quickly darkness came on this side of the Front Range. Slocum wanted to keep on but knew that was not possible now. He had to eliminate the dry-gulcher behind them or be dogged the entire way over the mountains.

The attack seemed wrong for a man like Bear Zacharias. Zacharias lacked subtlety, and an ambush required a certain amount of patience along with sheer sneakiness. The bounty hunter would march up and punch out someone but was not likely to cut him down from hiding.

Slocum saw a small pull-out area used by other travelers and decided to risk this as a camp for the night. There was a small pool of crystal-pure water and the possibility of finding firewood nearby. He reined back, calmed the mules and then jumped down.

"Set up camp," he ordered Maggie. "I'm going to find our friend back there and settle his hash." He drew the Winchester from the saddle sheath and levered a round into the chamber.

"Wait, John, wait!"

He looked over his shoulder. Rachel came up.

"Let me go with you," she asked.

"You'll be safer staying here," he said. "I don't know who's out there. It might be Larson, or it might be Zacharias." He might have mentioned his old army commander to the young woman, for all the recognition registering on her face. "Until I find out for sure who's there, I don't think I can make any good decisions on how to get rid of him."

Slocum knew a bullet would take care of Zacharias as easily as it would Larson, but he had to know why they were after the women. Of the two, he suspected Larson was more likely the sniper. It was the kind of cowardly attack he expected from the man.

"I want to go," Rachel repeated.

"And I said to stay here. I'll let you know what I find." He stuffed a handful of rounds into his shirt pocket, then set out on their back trail to find the unseen sniper.

Slocum was so intent on finding their attacker, he never heard Rachel's soft steps following him.

7

Darkness wrapped around Slocum like a shroud. He shivered a bit as wind cut at his face and hands. Gripping his Winchester tighter, he moved to the side of the tracks where he had just driven the wagon and waited. Slocum had been a sniper during the war and had learned patience. Sometimes waiting as long as six hours for a single shot at a Yankee officer, he had been one of the best snipers the Confederacy had. Now that patience seemed to evaporate with the cold wind.

He thought he heard someone moving behind him. Slocum edged around and backtracked but saw no one. A flash of irritation passed. He had been jumping at shadows ever since he had spotted Bear Zacharias. Slocum was not afraid of any man, but if there had to be one that put fear in his heart, the bounty hunter was it.

Slocum waited a few more minutes but the sounds were not repeated—if Slocum had actually heard anything at all. He turned back down the road. There was no question someone had sent more than one bullet winging toward him. No phantom, no imagination, only hot lead sailing through the air intending to kill him. The darkness was almost absolute by the time he reached the road leading up into the mountains and over the pass. Slocum eyed the high canyon walls, hoping someone might outline himself against the bright stars shining so far above.

Nothing.

Slocum kept moving, wondering if he was on a wild-goose chase. It seemed incredible that Zacharias could have beaten them to the foothills. If the bounty hunter had ridden that hard, he would have passed them on the road and would not have bothered with an ambush. Whatever else he might be, Zacharias was straightforward. He would bang his hard head against a wall to knock it down rather than go around.

Soft sounds ahead alerted Slocum that someone waited near the road. He looked up into the rocks and saw movement in a rocky niche. There had been more than one bushwhacker. Slocum grimly advanced, ready for a gang of ambushers. That meant Zacharias was not their attacker, since the bounty hunter always worked alone. But Larson might have recruited some owlhoots from Denver saloons to join him.

Or it might be a gang of outlaws intent on robbing prospectors heading to the silver fields on the other side of the mountains. If so, they had given up mighty easily. This piqued Slocum's curiosity as well as raised his ire. He wanted revenge for nearly getting his head blown off.

The soft movement ahead alerted Slocum that he was getting close. Carefully advancing did not give him the upper hand. A shadow rose in front of him and rushed forward before he could squeeze off a round from his rifle. Grappling with the man proved even harder than Slocum had expected, and he had been ready for a fight.

Strong hands went to his throat, cutting off his air. Slocum used the pain in his back from the sharp rocks cutting into him to focus his anger and muster his strength. With a huge surge, he threw his attacker to one side. Slocum came to his knees in time to see the flash of starlight off a long knife.

He reached out in time to grab the man's brawny wrist and keep the knife from gutting him. Slocum twisted hard enough to force the man to drop the blade. Still on his knees, Slocum kept twisting and pulled the man around. He expected the attacker's body to hit the ground hard. Instead, the man allowed himself to be pulled over, rolled and wrenched free of Slocum's grasp.

Like a shadow, the man vanished into the night. The entire fight had lasted less than a minute and had been done in absolute silence. Slocum drew his Colt Navy and waited for a sound to give away his fleeing assailant. All he heard was the wind. For the first time, he put serious credence in having been attacked by ghosts.

Then he spotted the feather on the ground. Slocum touched the broken eagle feather, held it up and studied it in the bright starlight shining down directly from the narrow slice of sky above.

"Arapaho," he murmured. He had been wrestling with an Arapaho brave. Slocum looked back up on the sheer rock faces of the canyon walls on either side of the road. If an Arapaho lookout still crouched up there, the entire band knew he was alive and that the brave had failed to kill him.

Slocum tried to remember if he had heard any talk of Arapaho raiding parties in the area. He had not been in Denver long enough to speak to men coming out of Mosquito Pass, but there had been no gossip about Indian unrest. This might be a renegade band out to loot and kill.

It didn't matter to Slocum who they were or why they wanted to lift his scalp. Adding the Arapahos to the list of owlhoots after him and the wagonload of women weighed Slocum down even more. Zacharias, Larson, Arapahos. What had he gotten himself into?

Slocum might have left the four women on their own

once they started up into the pass, but now he dared not do it. Even Maggie, in spite of her assertions to the contrary, could not drive the mules and fend off a band of renegade Indians. He had bitten off more than he could chew, but now Slocum had to chew—fast.

He scouted a little more but found no trace of the Arapaho warrior who had attacked him. This did not surprise him much. This was Arapaho land, and they were expert at moving through it without leaving a trace that even an expert tracker could find. Slocum pressed his back against one cold, rock canyon wall and studied the distant wall where he thought the rifle fire had come from earlier.

After a half hour, he gave up. The Arapahos were his equals when it came to patience. If one sat up in a shallow cave, he did not betray his presence to anyone below, including Slocum. Deciding it was safe enough, Slocum went to the road and studied the tracks. Enough dirt blew across the rocky roadbed to let him see the traces left by his wagon. Slocum thought he found marks indicating that another wagon had passed by earlier in the day. Otherwise, no tracks showed.

He stood in the road and peered back downhill, wondering if anyone followed. This was the only road over the high pass, so prospectors and would-be miners all came this way from Denver on their way to Leadville. The flood of men hunting quick wealth was nowhere to be seen.

Neither was Zacharias or Larson—or the Arapahos.

Feeling the need for moving on but knowing it wasn't possible until dawn, Slocum decided to return to the wagon. Protecting the women took on more importance than ever. As he retraced his path, keeping close to one canyon wall to safeguard himself from detection as much as possible, Slocum felt as nervous as a long-tailed cat next to a rocking chair. It was this sensitivity to any unusual sound that alerted him of the Indians ahead, between him and the four women at their camp.

Slocum dropped to his belly and wiggled forward, more intent on scouting than taking out the Arapahos. He sucked in his breath and held it when he saw a dozen Indians huddled together. They spoke in low tones that mingled with the wind and came to Slocum in an unintelligible muddle. He knew enough Arapaho to get by but could not understand what these warriors discussed so heatedly.

They were decked out as hunters and not as a war party, but this did not make them any less dangerous. Now and then one turned and pointed up the road toward Mosquito Pass. Others immediately shook their heads and pointed north, into the tangled maze of canyons forming the Front Range.

Slocum was taken by surprise when one jumped up and ran off, his moccasins making only soft whispering sounds as he moved. The night swallowed up the brave, leaving the rest behind. Slocum wanted to take off and get back to camp, but he dared not move with so many hunters this close. Most carried rifles, but two held bows, with quivers of arrows slung over their shoulders. This told Slocum they were not a completely prosperous band or all would have had rifles. That made them even more dangerous.

What Arapaho would pass up an easy target if he could get a rifle for little risk?

The days of Arapahos taking slaves had passed, but Slocum did not want to risk the women's lives. He thought their honor had long since been compromised, but he wanted to avoid having them raped and then killed.

He, too, wanted to avoid being killed.

The Arapahos continued the discussion—argument?— for another few minutes. When the one who had left earlier returned, this provoked the entire band to split into two groups. One hurried off to the north, and the rest followed the returning warrior up along the Mosquito Pass road.

Slocum lay on the cold ground for another few minutes, waiting to see if any of the Arapahos would return. When none did, he got to his feet and wiped the sweat from his forehead. In spite of the chilly night air and the brisk wind, he had been sweating at the thought of taking on so many warriors.

He hurried back down the side road to the camp and was glad to see that the women had not started a fire. The scent of burning wood carried on the wind for miles and would have alerted the Arapahos.

"I've got some bad news," Slocum started when he saw Comfort and Maggie coming to greet him.

"Where's Rachel?" demanded Maggie.

Slocum fell silent, a cold lump forming in his gut. "What do you mean? Isn't she her with you?"

"She followed you," Comfort said anxiously. "We thought she was with you."

"I ran into an Indian hunting party. They might have been responsible for potshotting us out on the road, but Rachel wasn't with me when I spotted them."

"She lit out after you when you left camp," Maggie said.

Slocum started to tell the redhead how he had chased Rachel back, then stopped. Without a word, he started searching the ground around the camp until he found Rachel's small footprints leading off into the dark in a direction different from the one he had taken. She might have thought to circle and join him closer to the road. For what reason, he couldn't say.

"John, what are you going to do?" Comfort sounded distraught over her friend's absence. Slocum reckoned she had good reason to be worried this time.

"Find her," he said. He left the blonde behind by their

wagon as he tracked Rachel through the night. The going was hard, but Slocum was good and Rachel had made no effort to conceal her tracks.

Less than a mile along the trail, Slocum stopped and stared at what the ground told him. He sucked in his breath, held it until his lungs began protesting, then let it out in a slow gust. Rachel's small tracks mixed with others, which went off at an angle to the direction she had taken. Hers vanished entirely, telling Slocum she went with those crossing her path.

The tracks mingling with the dark-haired woman's were made by Arapaho moccasins. Slocum suddenly realized what the returning brave had told the others he had been spying on and why they had split and gone off so quickly. The Indians had caught Rachel and taken her to their camp, wherever that might be.

Slocum returned to camp. He had thought the news he had started to tell the women before had been bad. Now he had *really* bad news.

8

"What's wrong?" For once, Maggie didn't sound angry. This time she sounded all choked up. "What's happened to Rachel?"

"The ambushers we got away from out on the road were Arapahos," Slocum said, not seeing any reason to sugarcoat the problem. "I ran across a couple of them, but they got away. That means they know we're still here."

"But Rachel . . ." Elizabeth appeared to be the most concerned for her friend. "Do the Indians have her?"

"As close as I can tell, she didn't listen to me when I told her to stay in camp. Rachel lit out, maybe thinking to travel fast and circle to come up behind me once I reached the main road. What she figured on doing then, I don't know. The Arapahos got her before she reached the road, or so it looks from the tracks I found. They surrounded her. She never had a chance."

"What are you going to do?" Maggie asked, the edge coming back into her voice, as if Rachel's problem was his doing.

"There are at least ten Arapahos in the party. It's not a war party, so they might have been out hunting when they spotted us. Pickings along the pass road might be good for them with so many inexperienced prospectors heading over the mountains to Leadville."

"Those heathens have her," Elizabeth said, stunned. "There's no telling what they will do to her."

"They might let her go," Slocum said, "but I wouldn't count on it."

"You did this. You—"

Slocum cut off Maggie before she could get rolling with her stinging denunciation.

"I didn't do a damned thing," Slocum raged. "She tried to follow me. Who knows why, but I told her to stay put. She didn't. That's the simple fact of it. The mess she's in is all her doing."

"You can't leave her in their clutches," Elizabeth said.

"No, no I can't," Slocum admitted. "There's nothing one man is going to do against so many warriors. If I head back to that town we left, I can get the marshal to call up a posse. Or maybe I can find a fort and get some cavalry troopers into the field. Fort Junction is probably the closest."

"Fort Junction!" cried Maggie. "That's nothing but a bunch of sod houses filled with starving soldiers."

"If I don't find help in either of those places," Slocum went on relentlessly, "I'd have to ride all the way to Denver to find an Indian agent who knows how to parley with the Arapahos, and there's no way to tell which band is responsible. These might be renegades off a reservation or just hunters."

"Denver?" Elizabeth sounded stunned at the idea of going so far to get help. "You can't do that. That's miles and miles away! If you let those red devils keep Rachel that long, there's no telling what they'll do to her."

"She cozied up real good to the bounty hunter. Might be she takes to being a squaw," Slocum said, still angry. As soon as the words left his lips, he regretted saying them. He took a deep breath and said, "I didn't mean that. We're all in hot water out here. Trying to get over the mountains was a big mistake."

"No, it wasn't!" protested Maggie. "We have to get to Leadville or we'll be snowed out until spring."

"You want to leave Rachel?" he asked, taking no pleasure in how he forced untenable choices on the red-haired woman. "If you go on, you might make it to Leadville, but we'll be taking a powerful lot of time fetching help and then finding Rachel."

"Will they harm her?" asked Comfort.

Slocum hesitated. He had shot off his mouth enough and gotten the women upset. Then he said, "Probably. There's no reason for them to take her back to the reservation as a squaw when the Indian agent comes through every now and then. There'd be questions none of the Arapahos would want to answer about her."

"Then we have to save her," Maggie said positively. "What do we do?"

"We?" Slocum almost laughed. " 'We' do nothing except drive back to get help."

"What about the bounty hunter?" Comfort asked uneasily. "I'd be in trouble if he catches sight of me. Big trouble, maybe bigger than Rachel's predicament. There might be a noose waiting for me back in Kansas City."

"You'll have to keep under cover or stay at the camp where you hid out before." Slocum saw how complicated this was becoming. The more he thought on it, the less chance he saw for success in doing any of the things the women expected. Rescuing Rachel was chancy at best. Returning to town put Comfort in danger. And if he left them here and rode straight back, they might be discovered by the Arapahos. The Indians had to know a white woman would not be wandering around alone in these hills.

What would they do? Have their way with Rachel, then

kill her and hightail it? As much as Slocum hated to admit it, that was the most likely end to this reckless trip over Mosquito Pass.

"We'll stay here while you go for help," Maggie said firmly. "You can travel faster alone than with us. That'll keep Comfort out of trouble and give you the best chance for returning with a posse."

"No!" protested Elizabeth and Comfort as one. They looked at each other. Somehow, Elizabeth got appointed as spokesman for the pair. She said, "John, it'll take too long. It might be a couple days before you can get back, and our reception in that town wasn't such that you can depend on the marshal to do anything to help us."

"He's a lawman. It's his job to protect citizens, whether he likes it or not," Slocum said, already getting his horse ready for the trip. If they all went back, he could leave them. Let Comfort dodge Zacharias and let the other two complain about not reaching Leadville this season. Slocum knew now that his reach had exceeded his grasp when he agreed to squire the women over the pass.

"How long before you think you can be back?" asked Elizabeth. She came to Slocum and put her hand on his leg. Her brown eyes stared up at him. Slocum tried to read what went on behind those big brown eyes but couldn't.

"As fast as I can," he said. He looked around. Maggie stood beside the wagon, looking worried. "Keep low," he told her.

Maggie grumbled something about her trunk that he could not understand. He saw no reason to waste time asking her to speak up. Slocum wheeled his pony around and set off at a brisk walk, not daring to go faster in the dark. The light from the stars was bright, but not bright enough to illuminate the road enough to ride faster.

As he went around a bend to head for the main road, he reined back hard, thinking he saw a ghost. Then he realized it was only the starlight shining off Comfort's golden hair. The woman stood in the middle of the road, arms crossed just under her ample breasts. From the set of her body, he wondered why she wasn't also tapping her foot angrily.

"Get on back to camp or they'll nab you, too," he told her.

"You can't go, John. You can't."

"There's no way I can take on a dozen Arapaho braves," he said.

"Every time you talk about them, the number goes up."

"Doesn't much matter if it's two or twenty," Slocum said, dismounting. "There's plenty more of them than of me."

"Are you saying those heathens are a match for you?" She moved closer. Slocum began feeling uneasy at her nearness. Comfort was a lovely woman, and he found her overpoweringly seductive.

"Yep, that's exactly what I'm saying. They know this territory, and I don't. Besides that, they have the advantage of holding Rachel as a hostage. It's easier to kill her than to rescue her."

"Don't go up against them with a frontal assault," Comfort said. "Sneak in and rescue her. You're good, John. I know it."

Slocum noticed the blonde had moved even closer to him. In spite of the cold wind blowing from the upper elevations, her blouse hung open, giving him a good view of her breasts. In the starlight they gleamed like silver. Combined with the cascades of her palomino golden hair, she seemed more metal than human flesh.

Any such thought quickly vanished when Comfort threw her arms around his neck and pulled him down so she could kiss him. Those breasts that had captivated him now crushed warmly against his chest.

"This isn't—" he started.

"I'm convincing you, John," she said, breathing harder. Comfort's fingers worked to get his gun belt off and his fly unbuttoned. Any pretense he might have made about not wanting her vanished when she gripped his manhood and tugged its rigid length toward her.

Comfort hiked her skirts and hooked her slender legs around his waist, pressing her most intimate region into his fleshy staff. Slocum groaned as she wiggled about and then found the precise spot they both wanted. She rose on tiptoes and then dropped down. As she lowered her body, he sank deep into her heated interior.

Surrounded by Comfort's body, Slocum felt a little weak in the knees. As he dipped down, she followed, then rose quickly, denying him the warm, moist chamber. Before he could protest, Comfort wiggled around again and once more Slocum sank far up into her clinging, warm sex.

Her arms held him close, but Slocum worked away enough to bend over and kiss her exposed breasts. When he began licking and nipping at her tender slopes, Comfort leaned back, trusting him to support her fully. This forced her groin down into his and allowed him to frolic between her breasts. His tongue ran up one slope and then slipped down the other, taking time at each crest to toy with the hard nubbin of flesh he found there.

Slocum knew Comfort's nipples were taut because of him rather than the cold. As he pressed his tongue down hard onto one, he felt her heart hammering away. He sucked in the tiny pebble of flesh and rolled it around with his tongue, then nipped down harder with his teeth.

As he did, an earthquake of desire passed through the woman's entire body. Comfort gasped and began to shake like a leaf in a high wind. Slocum felt her inner muscles clamping down spasmodically all around his hidden length.

"Oh, yes, yes, John, yes, don't stop. Please, no, you can't stop!" she moaned.

He held her closer, making sure the blonde did not get away from him. Running his hands around her and cupping her firm, round rump, he lifted her. Comfort quickly locked her ankles behind his back. This forced her entire weight down on the fleshy rod stuffed all the way up into her tender interior.

Slocum began bouncing her up and down, relishing the movement of the woman's body all around him. Her naked breasts bobbed and her face, upturned to the sky, showed only intense pleasure. This sparked Slocum's desires, and he knew he could not hold back much longer. He moved her up and down a few more times and then gave up all pretense of self-control. He bucked like a stallion and then spilled his seed.

The hot rush set off Comfort again. And then she lowered her legs to the ground. For a moment, she needed Slocum's support, then she got her skirts down and straightened to look him squarely in the eye.

"Rewards usually come after you've done something to deserve them," Comfort said. "This time you got yours before you rescued Rachel."

Slocum tucked himself back in, then buttoned Comfort's blouse for her.

"Let's hope it wasn't the condemned's last request," Slocum said, knowing it was likely to be. He was a fool for taking on an entire Arapaho party of braves, but there did not seem to be any other way of saving Rachel.

She had to be plucked from the hunters' grasp soon or she would end up as buzzard bait. Slocum had known it the instant he saw she had been kidnapped but had not admitted it to himself.

"Maybe not a *last* request," Comfort said. "Do a good job and let's consider it a down payment." She stepped up and kissed him passionately, then turned and lightly ran back toward the camp.

Slocum cursed himself for a fool, then headed out to find the Arapahos and their beautiful captive.

9

Slocum had known deep in his gut that he had to act to rescue Rachel himself rather than finding help from the cavalry or the law. Slocum had known that, but now it looked—and felt—as though Comfort had changed his mind with her alluring ways. That rankled as much as the notion that he was going to end up filled with bullets and Arapaho arrows.

Slocum rode back to the main road that lead up and over the mountains and looked downhill, toward distant Denver, civilization and personal safety. But hightailing it now doomed Rachel if he took that road. Slocum turned his pony's face uphill and rode slowly, listening for any sound that would alert him that the Arapahos were ahead. Less than ten minutes of riding brought him to a spot where brush along the road had been crushed.

Any passerby might have done it, but Slocum had to check. An errant, drunken prospector on his way to Leadville might have weaved off the road and broken the limbs on the low-growing brush, or it might have been Rachel's way of marking the trail. He had tried to picture where the Indians might have taken her. Tracking her from where she had been taken would have wasted precious time. From the look of the cut-up ground around the bush, Slocum had gambled and it had paid off.

This was Rachel's trail. Slocum smiled grimly when he saw definite proof. A piece of her dress had caught on a thorny limb. He peered into the darkness and started following the woman's tracks, his horse trailing behind. Slocum had gone less than fifty yards when he got a prickly feeling at the back of his neck.

The trail definitely went straight up a branching canyon. Slocum figured the Arapahos had their camp there and had made no effort to hide that fact. They were either innocent hunters with no reason to hide or their arrogance prevented them from believing they might ever be hunted. He saw no evidence that any of the warriors had left the path to lay an ambush for unwary trackers.

The feeling of danger grew until Slocum wanted to scream.

Slocum walked another few paces, then stopped and listened hard. He heard nothing from the canyon ahead, but from behind came the faint sounds of breaking twigs. Slocum looped the reins of his horse around a fallen tree limb, then drew his six-shooter and started circling to see who followed him.

He held the high ground and had reached the point of having to do something. He risked his scalp for Rachel and knew it was only out of guilt. Slocum had failed to protect her and now had to save her through stealth. His finger curled around the trigger, but Slocum forced himself to be calm. He knew what was at stake shooting this close to the canyon mouth where the Arapahos camped.

Slocum found a ravine, jumped into it and waited. Noise of someone—or something—moved closer along the trail he had already followed. Slocum leveled his six-gun and aimed at the spot where his tracker would appear.

"Son of a bitch," Slocum muttered when he saw Bear Zacharias. The bounty hunter blundered along like a bull in a china shop, making no effort to stay quiet.

Whatever skill Zacharias lacked in moving silently through the night, he made up for in other instincts. The bounty hunter stopped, turned and faced Slocum as if he could see him. Before Slocum could call out to keep the mountain of a man from doing anything stupid, Zacharias lifted a shotgun and fired.

Heavy buckshot ripped through the branches just above Slocum's head. Zacharias let loose with the second barrel of his gun, but the shell was bad. A popping sound produced only smoke and lead shot rattling along the barrel to fall to the ground.

"Dammit! Cheap shells!" Zacharias bellowed.

"There are Arapahos ahead," Slocum called. "Stop shooting!"

"Who's there?"

Slocum hesitated. He had no love for Zacharias and knew the bounty hunter would recognize him instantly. Slocum had a good shot and thought he ought to take it. But Rachel! He endangered the woman's life if he shot it out with Zacharias.

"Slocum. But we got to—" Slocum ducked when the bounty hunter reloaded his double-barreled shotgun and cut loose with more buckshot. The bounty hunter was not going to stop until he killed Slocum. Or Slocum ended the contest.

Backing off, Slocum clambered to the top of the ravine and headed for Zacharias. The bounty hunter remained in the sandy-bottomed arroyo, cursing a blue streak and stuffing new shells into his shotgun.

"Come on out, Slocum. I got a score to settle with you. You left me for dead, and I'm not gonna make the same mistake with you."

Zacharias lurched along, his heavy shotgun swaying back and forth like the head of a striking rattler. Slocum waited for the bounty hunter to pass by him. He aimed at the back of the man's shaggy head, knowing he could end it fast.

He had the chance to kill Zacharias again, and again Slocum hesitated. Whatever he was, he was no back-shooter. If any man deserved being cut down, it was Bear Zacharias. But Slocum couldn't do it.

"Where you at, Slocum? You got a wanted poster on your head, don't you? How much was it? A hundred? Fifty dollars? A goddamn dime? Don't matter to me. I'll take your scalp in, too, just for the hell of it."

Slocum got his feet under him, turned and jumped. He lifted his pistol and brought the butt down as hard as he could on the back of the bounty hunter's head. The sick crunch as metal hit bone echoed along the ravine. Zacharias staggered forward and discharged both barrels into the ground in front of him. But Slocum saw he had not knocked out the bull of a man. He took three quick steps after Zacharias and hit the bounty hunter again. Hard.

This time he drove Zacharias to the ground. Blood oozed from both wounds, showing he hadn't killed the bounty hunter. Slocum doubted it was possible to kill the man by hitting him on his thick skull. Bear Zacharias was too much like his namesake. Slocum had shot a grizzly between the eyes at point-blank range and the slug had bounced off, infuriating the bear further. The only way he had escaped being mauled was to pretend he was dead. The bear had shaken him and clawed him a mite and then dropped him to find other prey.

Slocum stood over Zacharias, looking at the man's writhing body. Maybe the same tactics would work here.

Kicking the shotgun beyond Zacharias's reach, Slocum threw himself down on the ground and waited for the bounty hunter's eyes to focus again. The first thing Zacharias saw was Slocum sitting and holding his guts.

"You, Slocum, I'll—"

"You're too good for me, Zacharias. You got me good."

"I kilt you?" The bounty hunter shook his head as if checking to see if anything rattled loose. Slocum knew there wasn't much in there to be knocked free.

"No, not that. Wadding from your lousy loads hit me. Knocked me down. You got me, Zacharias." Slocum held his Colt Navy at his side where Zacharias could not see it. If the bounty hunter didn't go for his tall tale, a round or two in the man's chest ought to slow him down—for good.

"I did?"

"Won't do you any good, though, not with the Arapahos up the canyon."

"Injuns?"

"The ones who stole away the woman you're looking for. The blonde."

"What do you know of her? You throw in with her?"

It took all of Slocum's self-control to keep from thinking about how Comfort had given him such a send-off. He was not sure describing what they had done out there on the trail could be called "throwing in with her," but Slocum could worry about splitting such hairs later. He had to rescue Rachel and do it fast.

"The one back in town. Rachel. You find out about Comfort from her?"

"Naw, I already knew. That blonde's got a big trial ahead of her when I take her back. She's worth a thousand dollars."

Slocum blinked in surprise at that. Comfort had not been sure she had even killed her boyfriend. She must have killed him—and he must have had powerful friends or family for such a high reward to be levelled on her head. Slocum knew gunmen who had killed four or five men and carried only a few hundred dollars in rewards on their heads.

"The Arapahos have her in their camp ahead. Up the canyon."

"You tryin' to save her and get the reward for yourself?"

"Not any longer," Slocum said. "I don't think I can move. You broke me up bad. It feels all watery inside." He coughed a few times and spat, hoping this would give the illusion of a man dying from internal injuries.

"I'll pick up your worthless body on the way back," Zacharias said, getting to his feet. He took a few unsteady steps toward Slocum. Slocum lifted his six-shooter and waited to see if he had to shoot. Zacharias was still too dazed from being hit on the head to focus his eyes well.

"Don't leave me for those heathens to scalp," Slocum said, watching Zacharias closely. "I'd rather you turned me over to the law for the reward."

"Some good would come from your miserable existence, Slocum," declared Zacharias. "Up that way?" He pointed in the direction of the canyon.

"There," Slocum said, coughing again.

"Try not to die 'fore I get back. If you do, see you in hell, you miserable owlhoot."

"Good seeing you again, too, Zacharias," Slocum said, watching the bounty hunter's broad back vanish in the darkness. He got to his feet and knew he had to move fast. Zacharias would barge right into the Arapaho camp and devil take the hindmost. Slocum wanted to have Rachel out of the Indians' clutches by the time the bounty hunter distracted them.

That distraction could give Rachel and him the chance they needed to escape. Otherwise, it was likely to be a running gunfight with the Arapahos that Slocum knew he could never win.

Keeping pace with Zacharias proved easy. Slocum heard the bounty hunter lumbering along, not even trying to approach the Arapaho camp silently. Slocum sped up,

pressed into a canyon wall and hurried ahead of Zacharias.
The scent of a campfire came to him, followed swiftly by
the smell of tobacco and cooking meat. The Arapahos had
been successful in their hunt and were celebrating.

Slocum hoped they weren't celebrating using Rachel.

Keeping an eye peeled for a sentry, Slocum advanced
on the camp. The small cooking fires blazed merrily, forcing away some of the nippy cold night. The Arapahos'
horses nickered as he approached, but Slocum moved qui-
etly and took time to gentle the spirited animals. Then he
drifted like a ghost until he found a spot to spy on the
Indians, not ten feet from where six of them huddled
around a fire.

They spoke in low tones. Slocum strained to hear what
they said but could not. The other fire was being used to
fire-harden arrows. Those had to be the poorer relations.
They could not even afford the metal arrowheads traders
often sold and must have used their stone points during
the hunt.

Behind them in the dark hung four deer carcasses.

These were successful hunters. But where was Rachel?
Slocum knew he had not confused the trails, and he
doubted she could have avoided a band of hunters as as-
tute as these.

He felt time running out on him. Zacharias would burst
into the camp at any instant. Slocum had to find Rachel
and be ready to escape with her as soon as the bounty
hunter made himself known to the Arapahos.

Slocum had developed a sixth sense during the war. It
had kept him alive, and he obeyed its impulse now to
throw himself sideways. He slammed hard into a tree
trunk but saved himself having a hatchet buried in his
head. The Arapaho missed with his blow and fell to one
knee, off balance.

This was the only chance Slocum was likely to get. He
swarmed over the brave, driving his knee into the man's

hard gut. Slocum had hoped to knock the wind from the brave's lungs. Instead, he missed and only punched at his rock-hard belly. But he still had the element of surprise on his side.

The Arapaho had thought he would kill the intruder. Tables turned fast, and the Indian found himself pinned to the ground, Slocum's hands circling his windpipe. Gurgling, struggling for air, the Arapaho brave tried to break Slocum's grip. Kicking and thrashing about did not weaken the death-dealing pressure on his throat, so the Arapaho tried a different trick.

He raked his fingernails like claws along Slocum's forearm. Slocum recoiled, giving the Indian a chance. A small one. Slocum's grip was broken, but he still held the Arapaho down with his knees in a schoolboy pin. Slocum fell forward, his injured arm a bar across the Indian's exposed throat.

This time Slocum did not let up until the last vestige of life seeped from his victim's body.

Panting, he reached over and grabbed his six-shooter. He looked around to see if the fight had drawn any unwanted attention. It hadn't—because Bear Zacharias had made his entry into the Indian camp.

Shouts, shots, curses filled the air. The throaty roar of the bounty hunter's shotgun answered Arapaho rifles. Slocum looked around, desperately searching for Rachel. She might be dead. If so, he wanted to find her body rather than assume that she had been killed. He backtracked on the Indian who had attacked him, found evidence of a new, narrow trail to one side of the camp and followed it. Slocum almost stumbled over Rachel.

The woman was securely tied spread-eagle. From the condition of her skirts, he guessed he was too late to help her much more than freeing her.

"Slocum," she said dully. "You came."

"No time to talk," he said urgently. He yanked her

ropes off her wrists and ankles. "Can you stand? Ride?"

"I'll do whatever I have to," she said, her words life-less. The first hint of interest came when she heard Zach-arias's shotgun belch again. "Who's with you?"

"Your friend from town," he said.

"Who?"

"Never mind." He herded her along the path toward the corral where the Arapaho horses reared and whinnied in fear at the goings-on in camp. Slocum jumped and caught the bridle on one, pulling it down until he could control it.

"I've never ridden without a saddle," Rachel said, "but I'll try."

"No need," Slocum said, swinging up. He reached down, took her hand and pulled her up behind him. "Hang on to my waist. This is going to be one hell of a ride."

He used his strong legs to turn the horse, then drew his six-gun and put his heels into the Indian pony's flanks. The horse took off like a rocket.

Slocum didn't try to pace the horse but let it gallop flat out through the Arapaho camp, kicking up embers from the cooking fire and sending bright sparks high into the air. All around them the Indians fired wildly. And ahead Slocum saw the bounty hunter fighting off two braves.

Zacharias held his own, stronger than the pair of Arap-ahos. The bounty hunter had dropped his shotgun but didn't seem to need it at the moment. Slocum and Rachel flashed past and into the night, hearing the man's grunts and curses.

Slocum kept the horse galloping in spite of the danger of tripping and falling in the night. He did not want the horse to break a leg; neither did he want the Arapahos or Zacharias to catch up with them.

"You're leaving him to fight the Indians?" Rachel asked. Her voice came out flat and monotone, as if she knew she ought to be interested but could not work up enough enthusiasm to sound concerned.

"You attached to him? I told him Comfort was their prisoner. He's mighty high on taking her in for the reward on her head but didn't seem too intent on saving you." The last was a shot in the dark since Slocum had never mentioned that Rachel was being held captive.

"I wouldn't know about that," Rachel said.

"You and Zacharias hit it off pretty good back in town. You mean you didn't know he was after your friend?"

"No."

"What about Larson?" Slocum asked on impulse.

Rachel held on to him but did not answer. He might have been riding alone through the night on the rapidly tiring horse. Slocum reined back a mite, then slowed the horse to a walk so he could find where he had left his own horse.

He helped Rachel into the saddle on his, then followed on the tired Indian pony. She hadn't answered his questions and did not seem disposed toward making small talk.

Rachel did not even bother thanking him for rescuing her.

Slocum wondered anew what he had gotten himself into squiring the women over the pass to Leadville.

10

Slocum kept looking over his shoulder, uneasy at all that had happened. Bear Zacharias ought to be dead by now. For that favor, Slocum silently thanked the Arapahos, but they would not take kindly to anyone coming into their camp, killing at least one of their hunting party and then stealing a horse and a woman they had taken captive. Slocum did not know which chief led this particular band but thought he would be mighty angry.

Angry enough to track the woman and her rescuer to the ends of the earth for revenge, no matter that the Arapahos had already killed another intruder to their camp.

Glancing up into the inky-black night sky, Slocum wondered if the moon would be up anytime soon. The best he could remember, it was only a sliver past new moon, but even this dim light would help them along the trail faster. As bright as the stars in the diamond band of the Milky Way were, the light was too faint for easy riding along the rock-strewn trail. To make matters worse, wispy clouds whipped across the sky, further shutting off the pale light.

"Do you know where we're going?" asked Rachel. These were the first words she had spoken since Slocum had asked her about Larson.

"Yes, of course I do," Slocum said, almost preferring her silence to questioning his abilities. He had rescued her, and she had not bothered to even say a simple "thank you" for all his trouble. Now she came out and practically branded him an incompetent trailsman. "I came up this canyon earlier. The one branching to the right takes us back to the main road. We can be in camp within an hour."

"Which canyon to the right?" Rachel asked sullenly. "There're two."

Slocum had not noticed this when he was tracking the woman earlier. He dismounted at the junction of the three trails and tried to find his spoor or that left by Zacharias or the Arapahos earlier. He gave up after ten minutes, feeling the pressure of time wearing him down as well as Rachel's stony silence. The Indians would be breathing down their necks soon, and Slocum knew he had to cover as much distance as possible if he wanted to escape. Even then, it would be touch and go.

It wouldn't take any great skill for the Arapahos to find the wagon with the other women. There might yet be a fight that Slocum—and the four women—could not win.

"So?" Rachel sounded peeved at his inability to figure out the proper route.

"Look," he said, not bothering to check his anger. "I just saved you from getting killed. You don't think they were going to take you back to the reservation as some kind of princess, do you?"

"They didn't kill me, but that doesn't mean you weren't too late getting me out of there," Rachel said in a flat voice. "They used me. Over and over."

"I'm sorry about that, but as you can see, traveling in the middle of the night is hard. Tracking is even harder. If your dress hadn't torn on a thornbush, I might still be hunting for you." He wanted to lash out at her, tormenting her with how he had warned her not to follow him and how anything that had befallen her was strictly her fault. Slocum took a second to get himself under control. She had been through hell tonight and would be there again if he didn't get them out of the winding canyons and back to the road where they might enlist aid from prospectors and other travelers going to Leadville.

"Zacharias found me easy enough."

"I told him where you were," Slocum said, feeling a small glow of pleasure at his deception and how well it had worked. The bounty hunter's entrance into the camp had been everything he had hoped. The timing was a tad off for perfection, but Slocum had counted heavily on Zacharias's lack of subtlety. It had made rescuing Rachel easier than if he had gone into the Arapaho camp alone.

"Why?"

Slocum did not answer. Rachel spoke as though she considered it her duty rather than really wanting to know. He prowled about like a caged animal, hunting for any hint about which canyon to take. Both had narrow, rocky trails showing recent passage of many horses, both shod and unshod. He could not tell if they had all passed by at the same time, in a large group, or if they rode separately. The Arapahos might have coursed up and down the entire mountainous region hunting for the deer they had strung up at their camp. Who had ridden the horseshoed animals Slocum could not say. All the tracks were recent, but how recent he could not tell in the dark.

"This one," Slocum said, pointing to one canyon. He had no sense that either one was right, and that bothered him. Getting lost in the winding gorges of the Front Range might mean their death. Slocum had another situation to consider, as well. If they took too long getting back to the other women, Maggie might take it into her head to cross Mosquito Pass on her own. Patience was not her strong suit.

Rachel snapped the reins and got Slocum's horse

headed up the canyon he had pointed to. He almost called to her that he had changed his mind and she ought to ride into the other canyon, but appearing indecisive rankled him. All his dealings with the women were fraught with guilt.

It still bothered Slocum that Comfort might think he had gone to save Rachel because of what they had done out on the trail, rather than because Slocum had realized Rachel would be dead if he did not act quickly. From what he had seen, the Arapahos would have killed her long before the cavalry could have ridden in from Fort Junction. He had done the right thing, Comfort's seductive plea or not.

He was increasingly angry with himself over making good decisions for what might seem bad reasons. Slocum stared at Rachel for a moment, then vaulted onto the Indian pony and followed the dark-haired woman. A hard life had taught him to honor his first choices. Changing his mind usually got him into a passel of trouble. And right now, more trouble was the last thing he needed. He had already found more than his share of aggravation since coming into Colorado Territory.

They had ridden less than ten minutes when Slocum reined back. Rachel continued along the confined, twisting trail, oblivious to his stopping. Slocum cocked his head to one side and listened hard. If the Arapahos were already on their tails, he might not hear anything before a loud whoop of glee as the warriors killed him. But this was a faint sound, distant and indistinct but definitely not natural. Someone was back there.

Slocum thought about getting his Winchester from the saddle sheath, then changed his mind. Let Rachel ride on as a decoy. He would wait and see who dogged their tracks. It might be Zacharias, though how the bounty hunter had escaped the Indians was beyond Slocum's reckoning. That left only the Arapahos. To take them on again, Slocum wanted complete surprise when he attacked. He might not get more than a single chance.

"Slocum!" came Rachel's aggrieved voice. "This is a dead end. You led us into a box canyon!"

He cursed under his breath. Whoever followed must have heard as her words echoed back down the length of the steep-walled canyon. Worse, they knew Slocum had to fight like a trapped rat, unable to escape because of the box.

Slocum slid his six-gun from the cross-draw holster and waited. A figure rode up deliberately. From the occasional glint of pale starlight off gunmetal, Slocum saw that the man carried a rifle in the crook of his left arm, ready for action. But Slocum could make out nothing of the mysterious rider's features. The darkness become too intense when the thin clouds turned more solid as they drifted across the sky.

A single shot could decide the matter. This unknown rider was not an Arapaho, although the Indians might not be far back. Slocum hurried along the trail, found two tall rocks forming a narrow channel like a doorway, then got ready for the kill.

Lifting his six-shooter, Slocum aimed for the spot where the man would pass between the rocks. When his target did not appear, Slocum knew he had given himself away. He shoved his six-shooter back into its holster and lit out on foot, trying to circle so he could come on the unknown tracker from behind. It wasn't much of a plan, but it struck him as better than anything else he had done since leaving the Arapahos' camp.

He blundered along in the dark, then cut toward the trail, hoping he had passed the man coming so stealthily after him and Rachel. Slocum knew right away the man had guessed his trick and had backtracked a dozen yards. He knew it because he heard the sharp metallic click of a rifle's hammer cocking, quickly followed by the whine of a bullet sailing past his head.

Slocum dived for cover, wishing now he had his own rifle. He risked being hit twice more before he pinpointed his ambusher's position in the dark. Slocum knew better than to waste his ammo shooting at a shadowy target. He also wished he had his other six-shooter from his saddlebags. He might as well have wished for a mountain howitzer, because all he had with him was the single-action Colt Navy loaded with six rounds.

Poking his head out, Slocum aimed carefully and squeezed off a round. The shot brought immediate response. In rapid succession, three foot-long tongues of orange flame danced out of the rifle's muzzle, but these bullets went wide. Slocum fired again, but he did not have the feeling he had winged his assailant.

Slocum scrambled to his feet and tried to move around, to get behind the man again. Something betrayed him as he ran. One rifle slug took off his hat and sent him diving flat onto the ground. He skidded a foot, then twisted about and waited to see what happened. Let his attacker think he had killed him.

Would the man come to check his marksmanship? If he did, Slocum would ventilate him. But after a full minute of waiting, Slocum got to his feet and retraced his path. He found the trail and went up it a few yards. Brass crunched underfoot. Slocum touched one spent cartridge and almost burned himself. This was newly fired, but the rifleman was nowhere to be seen.

A cold hand grabbed at Slocum's heart.

Rachel!

He lit out along the trail, knowing he had forgotten one small detail when he tried to get behind their would-be killer. He had the man trapped in a box canyon—with Rachel.

When Slocum came even with cut in the twin rocks

where he had thought to ambush the man, he skidded to a halt. Advancing more cautiously, Slocum looked all around warily. He did not want to spring the very trap he had intended for another. But all he saw was the Indian pony trying to graze on some chaparral and not having a good time of it.

Swinging onto the horse's back, Slocum put his heels hard into the animal. The only thought that repeated endlessly in Slocum's head was *Rachel!* He had sent the armed man to her. She had a rifle, but he had no idea if she knew how to use it. Moreover, she might think anyone riding in her direction would be Slocum.

He had been too clever by half.

His head low by the pony's straining neck, Slocum raced along the treacherous trail. He knew the horse might stumble at any instant. If the horse did fall, it might be curtains for both of them, but he had to reach Rachel, no matter the cost. Slocum considered shouting a warning, then decided it would do no good. Rachel had heard the gunfire. That might be enough to put her on guard.

And if the unknown rider heard Slocum's warning, he would realize he had not cut him down.

None of it made any difference, Slocum knew. The pounding hooves ought to be enough of a warning for anyone who wasn't deaf and stupid. And the man had already shown he was not stupid enough to fall into Slocum's traps. If anything, he had made Slocum out to be the foolish one.

Dark figures ahead in the middle of the trail, both dismounted, faced each other, ignoring him. It looked as if they were talking—or arguing. Slocum tried to figure out which was which so he could come to Rachel's aid.

He was momentarily blinded by the flash from a six-shooter. One silhouetted figure hunched over. The gunman fired again. This brought the victim down to the ground. A third round finished the crime.

Slocum whipped out his six-shooter, ready to bring the owlhoot to justice—six-gun justice.

He reined back and jumped from horseback, his thumb pulling back the hammer on his Colt Navy. Slocum stumbled along a few paces, trying to keep his balance after such a swift dismount. He stopped and stared when he saw the details more closely.

Rachel stood with his spare Colt in her hand. She had fished it out of his saddlebags. He tried to remember if it had been loaded. Slocum did not think so. Rachel had retrieved his six-shooter, loaded it and then had used it methodically on her attacker.

From the way the woman held the gun, it was not the first time she had fired a six-gun.

"Thought you were dead," she said simply. Rachel lowered the hammer on the Colt. Slocum realized then how close he had come to taking a round from his own spare six-shooter. She swung the pistol around and handed it butt first to him.

Slocum took it without saying a word.

He turned from the impassive woman and knelt by the man all curled up in a ball on the ground. Slocum rolled the man over. The clouds above parted just enough to cast a ray of cold silver moonlight on the man's face.

Slocum looked up at Rachel and said, "You killed Larson."

"Fancy that," was all she said.

11

Slocum kept thinking how comfortable Rachel looked with his six-shooter in her hand. She had cut down Larson and never batted an eye. Slocum was more than a little glad that he had taken the pistol from her and put it back in his saddlebags out of her reach. He also made sure she rode at his side or ahead and never behind him. He should have been scouting the trail back to where the others camped, but he had long since passed trusting Rachel.

She was quiet, withdrawn, and he knew she could kill without remorse.

Slocum kept his head moving like a chicken pecking at grain. Looking this way and that while he rode, he felt as though he had turned into one giant raw nerve. Every sound, no matter how slight, spooked him. He saw shadows moving when there was nothing but the chill wind climbing down from the higher elevations. He even rode along with the eerie feeling that someone was watching him.

Who that might be went unanswered, and he shrugged it off as being too much on edge. Larson was very dead and buried under a pile of rocks to keep away the coyotes, at least until the voracious animals could dig down to the body. Zacharias ought to be dead, but Slocum had thought that before. And the Arapahos were nowhere to be seen. It was as though the earth had opened up and swallowed them.

That wore on Slocum's nerves the most. The Indians were out hunting. The number of deer hanging from the oak tree limbs in their camp showed that, but he also knew that they were hunting for more than game. Anything along the road over Mosquito Pass was fair game, too. He had robbed them of their captive and a horse, both crimes that would never go unavenged.

Slocum and Rachel took the proper canyon back to the main road and then downhill to the cutoff toward the camp and never spotted a single Arapaho brave. It might have been possible that they got spooked and ran back to their reservation, but Slocum had trouble thinking that. Revenge was too much a part of their makeup.

The only bright spot Slocum could find was how Maggie had kept the campfire low and banked so it wasn't visible until he almost rode over it. With such caution, he hoped the Arapahos—and everyone else on the women's trail—missed them completely.

"You're back!" cried Comfort, seeing Rachel. The two hugged, but Slocum saw all the emotion was on the blonde's part. Rachel smiled faintly and spoke to the others, then hastily excused herself. It might have been the horror of her captivity that made her this way, but Slocum thought differently when he saw that none of the other women looked surprised at her actions. They accepted Rachel as being standoffish. It was almost as though they feared her.

"Thank you," Comfort said, smiling almost shyly. In a lower voice, she added, "You can collect the rest of your reward any time you want."

"We've got to make tracks," Slocum answered. As pretty as Comfort was, he had to think with his head and not his balls. "Everything packed and ready to roll?"

"Why, I suppose. That's Maggie's job," Comfort said, a little confused at the question.

"I'll find out," Slocum said, pushing past Comfort. He felt a tiny tingle of desire as his arm brushed against her full breasts. He also saw the hot look Elizabeth gave him. Jealousy was not what he wanted to provoke among the women.

He had troubles enough.

"So you rescued her?" Maggie said, almost accusingly. Slocum expected such a reaction from her. The redhead lived up to the reputation of fiery-haired women, but Slocum was getting tired of it.

"At first light, we move on," he said. "Be sure everything's secure. The road turns steep within a mile."

"Wait," Maggie said, reaching out and catching his arm. "I . . . I can be a bit brusque. I'm really grateful that you brought Rachel back. You don't know what it means to me. To all of us."

"Just doing my job," Slocum said, wondering what the hell his "job" was, anyway. He acted out of a sense of guilt, not duty. And he certainly was not being paid. If anything, the four ought to pay him for the use of his wagon and team. He had won them fair and square from Voss.

At the memory of the mule skinner, Slocum uttered a low curse reflecting on Voss's dubious parentage and crude personal habits. To make it worse, Voss had gotten himself killed, probably by Larson. Slocum increasingly wanted that pleasure for all the trouble Voss had lost to him in the poker game.

Slocum pitched his bedroll near the fire, lay down and found he could not sleep. He stared at the clouds that alternately hid and revealed the sparkling cold stars above and listened for any sound that might alert him of an attack.

All he heard was the whining wind, the desultory crackle of the dying fire and Elizabeth arguing with Comfort. He could not hear what they said to each other but thought he was probably the cause of the quarrel. That did not make him feel any better as he eventually slipped off into a troubled sleep filled with circling buzzards of pure gold and burning hot desert sun.

When he awoke, he almost wished for the nightmare of being stranded in the desert. Sometime after he and Rachel had returned, the clouds had thickened and a light coating of snow turned the landscape lovely—and the roads even more treacherous. The women were already awake and eating a sparse breakfast. Slocum joined them. Comfort looked sideways at him, and Elizabeth only glared. Rachel had retreated into herself, and Maggie became even more the mother hen until Slocum could take no more of it.

"Into the wagon. We're pulling out right now." He heard them protest but did not care. Tying his horse to the wagon and seeing that the stolen Indian pony was likewise secured, he hitched up the team of mules and got the wagon slipping and sliding along the icy tracks on its way back to the main road.

"You're not turning around, are you?" asked Maggie. "A little snow isn't going to stop you?"

"We'll go on, for a spell," Slocum agreed. The thin icy layer of snow hardly slowed their ascent into the pass. The mules' hooves cut easily through the frosty layer to find solid ground beneath them, and the wagon wheels spun a mite but not enough to stop their progress. Even the savage wind from the higher elevations had died down, allowing the wan sun to give them some warmth.

In spite of the good signs, every mile he drove worried Slocum that much more. What had become of the Arapahos? He hoped they had hightailed it back to the reservation with their kill, but if so, a bigger war party might return to avenge the brave he had killed. And Zacharias had probably taken a few with him. The bulky bounty hunter had been a strong, violent man capable of tackling an entire barroom full of drunks. Killing two or three of the Arapahos should not have been impossible for a man as ornery as Zacharias.

Slocum snapped the reins and got the mules pulling a little harder.

All day he drove, avoiding what he thought were treacherous spots and keeping an eye peeled for pursuit by the Arapahos. He avoided the slick patches and saw nothing to warn him that the Indians were the least interested in scalping him or taking the women for slaves. Getting toward midafternoon, Slocum actually relaxed and began to enjoy the trip.

He enjoyed it until Maggie decided to come forward and begin her haranguing again. Slocum hoped that whatever miner married her already had gone deaf from too many underground explosions.

"We're starting to think about dinner," Maggie said. "Can you find a place to stop where we can cook something?"

"There's still an hour or more of sun," Slocum said. "It's best to keep driving until dark."

"We're hungry now," Maggie said, her voice colder than the mountain air around them.

"Then chew on something besides me. You were the one who wanted to get over the pass as quickly as you could. The weather's on our side right now. You *don't* want to see a snowstorm."

"It's not winter yet," she said. "But we are hungry now."

Slocum started to argue, then saw a signpost ahead.

"There's a stagecoach way station ahead. That might be a better place to stop for the night than out on the trail.

Might even be able to get some decent grub and save ours for later in the trip."

Maggie sniffed and made a face. "If you call what provender there is 'decent grub.'" She scooted around on the wagon seat and flopped over into the bed to tell the other three they were going to stop soon. What Slocum had not told her was the signpost told of the station being a mile farther up the road.

Way up the road. The elevation changed fast here, forcing the mules to put forth a real effort. The surefooted animals struggled along, making Slocum happy he had chosen to put the extra two into the team. Four would have made it eventually, but six assured a slow, steady climb.

As the wagon rattled over a ridge, Slocum saw the way station ahead. He heaved a sigh of relief. Too many of the stations were abandoned, especially this close to the winter snows. A wisp of white smoke curled from the chimney, showing that someone was either cooking or keeping himself warm. As he got closer, Slocum saw two horses in the corral.

"It's about time," Maggie said indignantly. "I thought you were going to make Leadville in one session."

"Looks to be at least one gent here," Slocum said. "Might be a pair of them. Divvy 'em up as it pleases you."

"What's that supposed to mean?" Maggie's lips thinned to an angry line. "You sayin' we—"

"Howdy!" Slocum called, cutting off Maggie's diatribe. He waved to the man poking his nose out the door. "You the stationmaster?"

"Reckon I am," the man said, coming out. He was younger than Slocum would have thought for a gent manning such a post. A man with a sure step and quick eyes drove over the mountains and left the tending of livestock and outfitting to older men or those disabled by their hard jobs.

"Be obliged if we could put our animals up for the night in your corral and get some hot victuals."

"No reason you can't do both," the man said, coming out. Slocum saw that he wore a six-shooter at his hip. Most stationmasters preferred shotguns for defense. Carrying around three pounds of iron on your hip at this elevation tired a man quick, too. Slocum jumped down and felt the strain on his lungs from the altitude.

"Slocum." He thrust out his hand. The man's grip was firm, but his eyes were on the women. Slocum couldn't help noticing that Elizabeth's brown eyes were similarly checking out the stationmaster. Her expression was virtually unreadable, but she stared at the man as though she had never seen a male of the species before.

"Kincannon," he said. "Walt Kincannon."

"Pleased to make your acquaintance," Slocum said. "You want to help the ladies down?"

"They your cargo?" Kincannon asked. He ignored the other women and grinned like a wolf at Elizabeth.

"Ask 'em. I'm sure they'll be more than happy to give you the whole story." Slocum looked around for the outhouse. Kincannon saw and pointed downslope a ways.

"Don't have no formal facilities," the man said, "and I recommend you know where you're goin' when you do. There's a cliff not ten paces farther on you surely do not want to fall over."

"Thanks," Slocum said, heading downslope from the cabin. He found it passing strange there wasn't an outhouse, but the rocky ground might have turned digging one into a chore.

On his way back to the way station, Slocum looked around, wondering what was wrong. He kept climbing the steep slope until he got to the cabin. Slocum frowned when he saw the slanted roof of a building in the other direction well away from the way station. Curious, he went exploring and found an outhouse nestled in a rocky draw where the digging was easier in the sandy bottom. Flies buzzed about, showing that the outhouse had been used. He went back to the way station and saw that the outhouse was hidden from view unless you were looking for it.

"You took so long, I thought you had fallen over the cliff," Kincannon said.

"Sitting in that driver's box all day made it a bit of chore," Slocum said. Kincannon laughed.

"Come on inside and eat," Kincannon invited. "The ladies have whumped up a meal for us. Not often do I get to eat a home-cooked meal. Gets kinda lonely."

"Reckon you see enough folks on this road, though," Slocum said.

"Nobody to stay with me, that's what I meant," Kincannon said. "All alone—'cept for the miners on their way over the mountains."

"Seeing so many fine-looking women come by must be a real treat," Slocum said, watching Kincannon closely. Something about the man did not sit well with Slocum, but he could not put his finger on what it was. His thoughts were interrupted when Elizabeth opened the door and called out to them.

"Come and get it 'fore I throw it to the hogs," she said, smiling. Her eyes glowed as she looked at Kincannon. Slocum wondered if she was just man-starved or if there was something about the stationmaster that he missed.

As he followed Kincannon inside, he wondered if there wasn't something he missed about everything dealing with the four women.

"Sit down and let us serve you," Elizabeth said. She began dishing out the food. It wasn't much, but it was hot and there was plenty of it.

"You're mighty generous, putting this much of your larder out for us," Slocum said, indicating the quantity of food. For a moment, Kincannon did not answer. Then he jumped as if Elizabeth had kicked him under the table.

"It's nuthin'. As I said, I enjoy the company. I surely do hope you'll stop here again when you come by."

"We're going on over Mosquito Pass into Leadville. Doubt we'll be back this way," Slocum said.

"I know, I know," he said, as if he didn't.

A silence fell as they all worked on their food. Slocum took seconds and considered going for more when he finished those, although his belly felt about ready to explode. In a way he envied animals like coyotes. A kill or two a week and they were happy. Dogs ate enough to tide them over for days on end, but he wasn't able to do that. He eyed what was left in the bowls, then pushed back from the table, shaking his head.

"Mighty good, but I've had my fill. Let's get everything cleaned up, then catch some shut-eye. I want to be on the road before dawn to make up for the time we lost here."

"I—" Elizabeth started to speak, then clamped her mouth shut. As if she summoned her courage, she looked at Rachel, then cast her eyes down before saying, "I want to stay here. With Walt."

"You what?" Maggie's question sounded more like a dog barking. "You have to come on with us. You can't stay here."

"I want to," Elizabeth said. She seemed mighty nervous about it. Slocum rocked back in his chair, watching the byplay, trying to understand it. The four had declared their intentions to find rich husbands in Leadville. If Elizabeth settled for a way stationmaster she had just met, she would be missing out on their big dream.

Moreover, Slocum couldn't rightly figure why she wanted to be with Walt Kincannon. The man was rugged enough and had the look of being able to do a day's work, but he was not rich. A woman as pretty as Elizabeth— and as talented—could have her choice of any man. Why come a quarter of the way over the Front Range to stay with a man not likely to see twenty dollars in a month's time, and this only during the summer months?

It made no sense.

"You can't stay. We made a deal. A pact," protested Comfort. "All of us together, because—"

"Shut up," snapped Rachel. Her dark eyes burned like twin coals as she glared at Comfort. "You talk too much." Rachel turned on Elizabeth. "You think on this. You should stay with us and not go off on your own. It's for your own good we're going to Leadville. You know that."

"I—"

"She's right," cut in Maggie.

Elizabeth refused to argue. What struck Slocum as odd was how silent Kincannon remained while the women tried to argue their friend out of staying. If he had been in Kincannon's boots, he would have laid down the law and let them know Elizabeth was staying.

None of it made a speck of sense to Slocum.

Slocum got up and went outside to fetch his bedroll and find a place to sleep. In the cabin didn't seem like too good an idea, not with Elizabeth and Kincannon likely to want some privacy. He waited and listened as Maggie harangued Elizabeth about going to Leadville to get rich. He could not hear what Rachel said, but the woman's intensity startled him. She had been so quiet to be so forceful now.

He harkened back to how she had cut down Larson so expertly. There was more to the women than met the eye.

And more than ever he wondered why he stayed. They were capable of getting over the pass without him, not that he had anything waiting for him back down the trail in Denver.

He fell into a fitful sleep with the thought "it makes no sense" rattling around in his head.

12

Slocum sneezed, rolled over and grabbed for his blanket. It had slipped off and was letting in wind whipping down from the distant pass. Slocum sat up when he heard shrill voices. Two of the women argued inside the cabin. Stretching, Slocum rolled his blanket and started preparing the mules for the day's travel.

Maggie stormed from the cabin, trying to slam the door behind her. The wind caught it and softened the loud crash. The fiery redhead glared at Slocum, then stalked off without a word. Following her came Elizabeth. The brunette looked uneasy but not as upset as her friend. Seeing Slocum, she smiled weakly and greeted him.

"Getting ready for the trip?" she asked, although it was plain even to a blind man that Slocum was feeding the mules and getting them into their harness for pulling the wagon.

"Is it going to be lighter today?" he asked. For a moment she did not understand. Then Elizabeth nodded. "Want me to get your gear out of the wagon?"

"I've already unloaded," Elizabeth said. "Last night."

Slocum started to say that the woman surely did move fast, once she made up her mind, but he held back the words. Rachel stood in the doorway, glaring at Elizabeth. Or was she also glaring at Slocum? He couldn't tell, and he didn't much care.

"There's no need to worry about me. I'll be fine with Walt," Elizabeth said. She looked around at the bleakness of the area. The way station had been built at the spot where the teams heading over Mosquito Pass tired the most, not because it was a decent spot to live.

"You going back to Denver?" Slocum asked.

"What? Why would I?"

"There's only a pair of horses in the corral. All the teams are gone. Makes me think Kincannon was fixing to leave for the winter. No reason to stay when the snow falls because nobody's going to travel the pass in either direction. Leadville gets cut off."

"I hadn't thought about that," Elizabeth admitted.

"There's not much you *have* thought through," Rachel said. She stormed after Maggie. Slocum felt as though he had been caught in the middle of a bad winter storm, ice pelting him from one direction and sleet from the other.

"Where's Kincannon?" Slocum asked.

"Still in the cabin," Elizabeth said. "He slept late. Gets real tired up here in this thin air."

Slocum frowned. He had felt winded the day before but had adapted fast to the altitude. Kincannon ought to have become accustomed long since. Before he could ask about this, Maggie and Rachel returned.

"We're leaving right now," Maggie said to Slocum. "Stop lollygagging and get to it."

Slocum bristled. He turned and faced her squarely. "I'm not your servant, and I sure as hell am not your slave. You ask politely or you go on without me."

"Why not?" snapped Rachel. "*She* decided to stay behind, after all we've done for her."

"Look, I—" Elizabeth clamped her mouth shut when Walt Kincannon came out of the cabin. The man stretched, yawned, scratched himself and then sauntered over to join the women. He put his arm around Elizabeth's shoulders. Slocum thought she cringed away a little, then forced herself to lean against him.

"You ladies all ready to go? Without breakfast? The little lady here, *my* little woman again, will be happy to whip up something for you."

"Get in," Maggie said, glaring at Slocum. "Please."

Slocum balked like one of the mules, then realized this was not the time to let the women go off on their own. Something about Kincannon's attitude bothered him—or was it Elizabeth's reaction to him? She had been a victim since he met her. He had rescued her from Larson and wondered if she needed rescuing now.

Then Slocum decided to forget it. She had made her bed. Let her sleep in it with Kincannon.

"All aboard," he called, climbing into the driver's box. He settled the reins, glanced over his shoulder and saw that both Rachel and Maggie had climbed into the rear of the wagon. He snapped the reins, then immediately shoved his foot against the front of the box and pulled back hard on the reins to stop the mules.

"What's wrong?" demanded Maggie.

"Where's Comfort?" Slocum asked.

The two women looked at one another, eyes wide. It was obvious they had been so wrapped up in their disputes with each other and Elizabeth that they had forgotten her.

"Kincannon?" asked Maggie. "What became of her?"

Kincannon shook his head and said, "Don't rightly know. Thought I saw her a couple hours ago, but I was hardly awake and passed it off as a dream."

"Saw her?" asked Slocum, fastening the reins and then jumping down. It began to feel to him as though they would never get away. The sun poked fiery fingers over a distant peak, promising a bright, clear day for travel. If they could ever get on the road.

"Didn't think much on it. Might be she was heading out to, well, you know."

"Go to the outhouse?" Slocum asked. That still bothered him that Kincannon had sent him in the wrong direction the day before. There was no reason not to use a perfectly good privy.

"I suppose we ought to look for her. She might have got herself into a world of trouble," Kincannon said. "This whole area's filled with timber rattlers."

Slocum said nothing to this revelation. He had yet to find anyplace in the Rockies not filled with timber rattlers, but the weather was so cold the snakes ought to be torpid. Comfort was wary enough to avoid stepping on one in the daylight when they were most likely to be out. Any rattler venturing into the cold night would find itself frozen stiff. If Comfort had left the cabin when Kincannon said, there wouldn't be a snake north of Albuquerque out wiggling about because of the low temperatures.

"You tell her to go downslope to do her business?" Slocum asked.

"Don't remember mentioning it to her at all," Kincannon said, moving away from Elizabeth and looking as though he was ready to go for the six-shooter in its holster.

"She must have overheard when you asked, John," Elizabeth said. She looked from Kincannon to Slocum, but it was Slocum she implored with those wide, fearful brown eyes to save Comfort.

"I'll see if I can pick up her tracks," Slocum said, starting downhill in the direction he had taken the day before.

"I'll come with you," Kincannon volunteered. "You ladies go on into the cabin and whump up some coffee. Reckon we're gonna need it somethin' fierce when we get back." He pulled his jacket around himself and shivered as a fresh gust of wind caught at him.

"You need your heavy coat," Slocum said, distracted. His keen eyes scanned the ground for any sign of Comfort coming this way. Although it was more guess than certainty, he started down a trail branching from the one he had taken.

"This goes right to the edge of the cliff I warned you about," Kincannon said. "You don't want to take a header there. Must be danged near five hundred feet to the canyon floor."

The trail quickly became steeper, forcing Slocum to turn to one side and slip down carefully. Now and then he lost his balance but kept his fall to a minimum. As he slid down the treacherous slope, he saw evidence that Comfort had come this way. Bits of her skirts had caught on rock and thorny bushes.

"If she went o'er the edge, she's a goner. You might as well come on back, Slocum." Kincannon had remained at the top of the slope, watching Slocum's perilous descent to the lip of the canyon.

"Got to be sure," Slocum said. He caught himself and edged forward to peer over the verge. Kincannon had been wrong. It was more than five hundred feet to the rocky floor. If anything, it could be twice that. Slocum had no fear of heights but a giddiness swept over him as he stared down to what would be death for anyone not sprouting wings.

If Comfort had come this way, she was long gone and long dead.

Still, something told Slocum not to give up so easily. He had not seen the blonde's body smashed on the ground below. Edging along, he found a spot ten feet away where the rock had given way. He dropped to his belly and peered over.

Twenty feet lower, on a ledge barely wide enough to

support her, Comfort clung to a rock for dear life.

"Comfort!" Slocum edged a bit farther out so he could look down at her. "Comfort! Are you hurt?"

The blonde turned her bright blue eyes up at Slocum. She sniffed loudly and shook her head. "No. But I'm scared to death!"

"Not yet," he told her. "You're not that scared."

"Yet," she added, trying to smile and make it into a small joke. "I almost died, John. Save me. Please, please save me!"

"I'll try," he said, seeing no way to reach her. The sheer rock face prevented anything other than a fly from crawling down to her. Even an eagle would have a time of it flying in past the craggy upthrusts of rock that had saved her life. She held on to one and a smaller stone spire had stopped her fall. Slocum saw how the rocky face was smeared with her blood where she had smashed into it, then rebounded to land on the ledge.

"I've been down here so long," she sobbed. "What time is it?"

"Dawn," he said, knowing he ought to keep talking to calm keep her but needing more to concentrate on a rescue. Slocum saw no way to climb down on either side and then work his way to her. She was stranded on a solitary ledge hardly two-feet wide and four-feet long. If Comfort had gone over the edge anywhere else, her next stop would have been the deadly floor a thousand feet below.

If Slocum failed to save her, she might still end up there.

"Hurry, John, I'm so tired. I don't know how much longer I can hang on." Comfort stopped talking for a moment, then said in a voice that floated up to Slocum like the whistling of a buzzard, "I'm so tired, so very tired."

"I'll get a rope. Don't let go, Comfort. Don't let go!"

Slocum inched away from the edge, then got to his feet.

Scrambling up the slope dislodged stones that cascaded over the edge. Slocum hoped none of them hit Comfort. She was in no condition to endure a hailstorm of rocks.

"Get a rope. A long one," Slocum told Kincannon. "I've got to go get her."

"Rope?"

"Look in the shed by the corral. There must be some there." Slocum was in no mood to argue. Kincannon set off, leaving Slocum to hunt for a place to secure the rope once the stationmaster returned. He found two likely boulders. Slocum decided on the larger of the pair by the time Kincannon returned.

"Don't know how much is here, Slocum," the man said, handing the rope over.

Slocum quickly fashioned a loop and secured it around the rock he had chosen. Tugging a few times showed it to be secure. He fastened the other end around his own waist, knowing how dangerous this rescue could be.

"When I call out, you pull us up," Slocum said.

"Dunno if I can pull both of you up," Kincannon said, rubbing his chin. "That's a mighty big chore."

"Try," Slocum said, sliding back down the slope. He tried not to send anymore rocks over the edge onto Comfort, but speed seemed more important to him right now. He walked to the edge and looked down, fearing that the blond woman might be gone. He heaved a sigh of relief when he saw how tightly she clung to the rock.

"John, I don't know how much longer I can stand it."

"I'll get you," Slocum said, turning to loop the rope around so he could walk down the rock face, letting the rough, dried-out rope slide under him. Even with gloves on, he felt the friction burning his flesh. He ignored the pain and carefully inched in Comfort's direction along the precarious ledge. When he got solid rock under his boots, Slocum let out a sigh of relief.

"I don't know if Kincannon is strong enough to pull

both of us up at the same time." Slocum untied the rope from around his waist and looped it around Comfort's body.

"Oh, that's nice," she said smiling at him. Comfort wiggled closer, her breasts brushing against his body.

"Later," he said.

"If you insist."

Slocum snorted in dismay at her. She was pale and trembling, yet she still flirted with him. He made sure the rope was tied with a double knot, then yelled to Kincannon to pull the woman up.

"Don't panic and you'll be fine," he told her as her feet left the ledge. Comfort started to thrash about, then settled down and tried to keep from being dashed against the rock face as Kincannon pulled her up, foot by painful foot.

Slocum experienced another bout of giddiness. He clung to the stony spire as Comfort had done, wondering how she had survived the fall and the ordeal of staying alive. He looked up and saw her feet vanish over the stony edge. It would be only a short time before the rope came back down and Kincannon pulled him to safety.

It couldn't happen soon enough, Slocum thought.

But it didn't happen at all. Slocum waited and shouted and raged, to no avail. He was trapped on the ledge as surely as Comfort had been.

13

Slocum inched to the far end of the narrow ledge. He vainly hunted for any way up the sheer face of the cliff. After twenty minutes of increasingly frantic searching, he gave up and reluctantly turned his attention in the only other direction he could go—down.

Dizziness hit him when he looked all the way to the bottom of the canyon. Closing his eyes and waiting for the giddiness to pass, Slocum regained his composure. This time he studied the area immediately under the ledge for any hint of outcropping. If he went down, he might find an easier path back up to one side of the ledge, though he doubted it. As a last resort, he might climb the entire way to the bottom of the canyon, hunt until he found a way back to the main road and the way station.

But that would take days. If he could even do it without falling. Slocum's ire grew into anger at how Kincannon had abandoned him. If it took him a year, he'd get even with the man for his betrayal.

Flat on his belly, Slocum reached down and grabbed a hardy bush growing out of a deep crevice. He tugged a couple times and thought it might hold him. Swinging around and lowering his body while hanging on to the bush for dear life, Slocum slowly descended. His toes sought any niche in the rock for support but found nothing. When the bush's roots finally began pulling free, Slocum knew he was a goner if he kept searching for a foothold.

Heaving hard, he flopped back onto the narrow ledge just as the bush pulled free. Slocum tossed the plant to the bottom of the canyon, silently wishing it good luck in finding a new place to take root. For a few seconds, it had been his salvation.

Slocum looked up at the top of the cliff, wishing Kincannon would poke his head over. One shot. That's all it would take to even the score. Slocum might not die happy, but he would take the treacherous Kincannon with him.

"John!"

He jerked around, his hand going to his Colt Navy. Slocum almost fell from the ledge as he turned. Abandoning his attempt to draw, he clung to the rocky spire behind him as he looked up to see Comfort's head.

"Get me off this ledge!" he shouted.

"I know, John, I know. We had to get a new rope. The one Kincannon used to pull me up frayed almost through. It would never have held your weight."

"Thanks for letting me know," Slocum said angrily. He stood, looking up for any sign that the woman wasn't just airing her lungs at his expense. Slocum was not sure if he was surprised when a knotted rope came sailing down. It swung just out of reach, but Comfort maneuvered it closer so he could grab hold.

"Who's doing the pulling?" Slocum asked.

"Kincannon, Rachel and me," the blonde answered. "Don't worry, John. We won't let you down."

Slocum foolishly cast a look below. It was a mighty long way down, if they did slip. But he had no choice but to trust them. If Kincannon or any of the women had wanted him dead, they could have left him.

Tying the rope around his middle, Slocum leaned back

a little and tested the rope. It was dusty and old. The other had looked to be newer. If it had given way, he worried how long this ancient hunk of hemp would last with his full weight on it.

Slocum took a deep breath, then called up, "Make it quick. I don't think the rope's up to the chore."

The rope jerked hard around him. Slocum kept his feet moving against the rock face. He went up fast at first, then slower and slower as Kincannon and the women tired. The lip of the canyon approached with agonizing slowness. Slocum's mouth turned to cotton. He wanted to pull himself up, but there wasn't a way to speed up the rise. His boots scratched the rock and then hit . . . nothing.

His feet kicked in midair, but his shoulder and chest were on solid rock. The rope cut into his back as Kincannon and the two women struggled to get him to safety. Just as his knees banged into the cliff face, Slocum lurched. The rope parted.

He slammed himself forward and grabbed frantically, his fingers cutting into the thin soil at the edge. Then both Comfort and Rachel caught his arms and pulled him to safety. He lay gasping for air, as much from the altitude as fright. Slocum wiped sweat off his forehead and said, "That was close."

"You're safe!" Comfort threw her arms around his neck and hugged him.

"Stop that," snapped Rachel. "If you hadn't gone sightseeing, none of this would have happened. You risked everything."

"Her life," Slocum said, interrupting Rachel. "Her life hung in the balance. It wasn't as if she fell over the edge on purpose."

Rachel's dark eyes flashed, and Slocum knew that wasn't what the woman had meant. She could have cared less if Comfort had died, but the notion that she had wandered off was somehow worse because it jeopardized some scheme the women had and which Slocum had yet to fathom.

Rachel spun and stormed up the hill. Kincannon hesitated a moment, then followed quickly. Comfort clung to his arm and laid her head against his chest until he was settled enough to return to the cabin.

"You saved me," Comfort said. "They would have left me. It was dumb going out like that, but I couldn't stand being around them any longer. I almost wasn't around anyone anymore."

Maggie bustled from the cabin. She tossed her head in their direction, and Comfort obeyed the silent command. Slocum knew he was about to hear some more from the fiery redhead about his failings. If she pushed him too much, she and the others could figure out how to reach Leadville on their own. He was at the end of his rope.

Slocum smiled without humor at the notion of how he had literally been at the end of his rope. Then his patience began to evaporate when Maggie started her harangue about how ineptly he had rescued Comfort.

"It was my life to risk," Slocum said, not bothering to argue with her. "And it's my life to live. Comfort, Rachel and Kincannon pulled me up. I'm grateful for that, but I sure as hell am not grateful for being taken to task every time one of you gets into a fix and I pull her out to safety."

Maggie's mouth opened, but this time no words came out. She looked like a trout washed up on the bank of a creek.

"I . . . I'm grateful, Slocum, really I am. It's just that—"

"That you can't come right out and say it?"

"No, it's Rachel. She was furious when Comfort disappeared like that. It put everything we're planning at risk."

"What might that be?" Slocum asked.

"Why, you know. Marrying rich miners." Maggie said the words and they hung like lead between them. Never had her lies been this obvious.

"Why are you so worried about what Rachel thinks?"

"She organized . . ." Maggie's words trailed off when she realized she had said too much. She cleared her throat and said louder, "Rachel is part of our group. One for all and all for one. We're sticking together."

"But she's in charge," Slocum said, marvelling at this revelation. Maggie had taken the attack every time something went wrong, but Rachel pulled the strings like a puppeteer behind the curtains. Slocum had ridden with cattle companies where the boss wasn't the top hand. He had learned to avoid situations like that because the real boss always had a goal different from that stated by the more vocal public leader.

"That's none of your concern," Maggie said sharply.

"No, it's not," Slocum agreed. He planned to get them on their way and then cut out. He had been shot at and almost killed by Arapahos, bounty hunters, kidnappers and now had been stranded on a tiny ledge after rescuing Comfort. That was more than enough excitement from winning the wagon, team and "cargo" from Voss.

Slocum did not believe in curses, but the wagonmaster had certainly died with one on his lips, damning Slocum for beating him at poker.

"We can't make any time today," Maggie said. "We'll stay until dawn tomorrow and then get back on the road."

"Suits me," Slocum said. His middle ached from rope burns, and his shoulders throbbed from the effort of pulling himself up the face of the cliff. Some rest and another hot meal or two would go a ways toward restoring his good humor. He doubted it would change his mind about staying with the women much longer on their excursion to Leadville bogged down with wealthy miners.

He went into the small cabin and saw Kincannon at the table, drinking steaming hot coffee from a battered tin cup. Slocum found himself another cup and poured some of the strong brew. He gulped half of it down. It burned his lips and threatened to blister where it settled in his belly, but the warmth restored him faster than anything else.

Staring at Kincannon caused more questions to pop up, but Slocum was past wanting answers. All he wanted now was to ride out and never see the four lovely women again.

"So Elizabeth's staying here with you?" Slocum asked after a second cup of coffee.

"Reckon so. Makes me one lucky fellow," Kincannon said.

"When are you heading back to Denver? Snows can't be too far off."

"Oh, I'm not sure. My duty's here . . ." Kincannon waved his hand indicating the way station. Slocum's gaze followed that movement. He wondered anew because of the lack of supplies. Kincannon pushed his luck staying here much longer. There might be food enough for another meal or two for all of them, but unless Kincannon was a better hunter than Slocum gave him credit for being, he and Elizabeth would be going hungry mighty soon.

"Think I'll rest up," Slocum said. "You mind?"

"Got chores to do," Kincannon said, as if he wasn't certain what they might be. He left, the door banging behind him. Slocum sat and stared after the man for a moment, then went and peered between the cracks in the wall to see that Kincannon spoke with Elizabeth. The two of them headed off, leaving Maggie and the other two women behind.

Slocum glanced over at the pile of the women's belongings brought inside for the night. He went to Elizabeth's trunk. Running his fingers over it, he came to a decision. Too many unanswered questions put his life at risk.

He opened the trunk and poked through the garments until he came to a stack of letters tied together with a wine-colored grosgrain ribbon. He untied the bow knot and leafed through the letters. All were from someone named Hamilton. The writing was crude, but Slocum got the gist quickly enough. Love letters from a beau in Leadville. He retied the stack and tried to arrange Elizabeth's belongings the way he had found them.

Slocum never hesitated when he moved to Maggie's trunk. It had been a bear to carry, heavier than the others. Forcing the lock, he stared in and saw the dresses and frilly undergarments he expected. What he had not expected was the arsenal.

He quickly inventoried four knives, four six-shooters, two Smith & Wessons of small caliber and two Colt .44s, as well as a Winchester rifle that had been disassembled and carefully stored in oilcloth. Alongside the guns he found enough ammunition to start a small war. He looked for letters from some lonely miner but found nothing.

Slocum quickly checked outside to be sure one of the women wouldn't come in and find him rifling through their trunks. Seeing the three of them sitting in the back of the wagon arguing told him he had a few more minutes to search. He went to Comfort's trunk and opened it. She had more clothing than the other two combined, all pressed down firmly into the bottom of the trunk. The bundle of letters, though, was different from Elizabeth's.

Six large stacks of letters attested to the blonde's interest in men. No man had written more than two, making Comfort's correspondence with half a hundred men all the more remarkable. Slocum scanned the letters quickly. Each of the men pledged undying love and offered to marry Comfort. Slocum had to wonder what she had written back. He suspected she had agreed somehow to marry each of the men, thinking to play them off against each other. That would appeal to her.

Or maybe she would decide, using the size of the man's bank account as her yardstick.

Before he could search Rachel's bag, he heard them coming, still arguing. He hastily closed Comfort's trunk and dived across the room, yanking out the chair and sitting down with his tin cup in hand as the three entered.

Rachel frowned at him but said nothing. Comfort smiled brightly and sat beside him. Maggie crossed her arms over her chest and glowered.

"What are you going to do now, John?" Comfort asked. "Can I join you?"

"I'm all tuckered out," he said. "I'm going to grab some sleep."

In a low voice only he could hear, Comfort said, "Let me join you. We won't get much sleep, though. I *promise*."

"Comfort," Maggie said sharply. "Let Slocum be. Come on, ladies. Let's clear out."

Comfort left reluctantly, her fingers lightly stroking across his arm as she trailed Rachel and Maggie from the cabin. The blonde blew him a kiss, then closed the door securely. Slocum sat for a moment, then went to finish his search. Rachel's large carpetbag might hold some clue at to their purposeful trip to Leadville, but what it might be he had no idea. Weighing it down was a medical text on human anatomy, with many of the pages dog-eared and turned down as though she had studied them repeatedly. Slocum hastily crammed the book back into the bag when he heard footsteps outside again.

Slocum spun, went to the fireplace and reached for the coffeepot hanging there. He looked over his shoulder, as though surprised when Kincannon came in.

"Thought you'd be asleep, Slocum," the stationmaster said.

"Too much noise in here. Think I'll take my bedroll off a ways and see if I can't get some peace and quiet," Slocum said.

"Good, 'cuz I got to do some work in here." Kincannon did not specify what that might be. Slocum downed what remained of his coffee and left, but he didn't go far. The women were once more in the back of the wagon. This time they sat in stony silence, pointedly ignoring one another. Slocum went around the cabin to the rear, hunting for a crack between the logs in the wall. Maintenance had been slack. He had no trouble finding a large hole to peer through.

He had not known what he expected to see, but he was not overly surprised that Walter Kincannon went through the women's luggage, just as he had done. Watching to see if Kincannon seized on something special, Slocum began to get edgy after five minutes. The stationmaster took nothing and showed no interest at all in the letters written by the lovelorn miners.

What he wanted remained a mystery as he searched but took nothing. Like Slocum, he left Rachel's large carpet-bag for last. Slocum moved to a different slit between the logs to get closer when Kincannon dug through the bag and stopped to examine something more closely.

Try as he might, Slocum could not get into position to see what interested Kincannon. When the man stepped away from Rachel's bag, it was closed and did not appear to have been rifled of anything important. Slocum wondered if Kincannon had slipped something under his shirt—or if he had simply found something that he had expected. Asking him was not likely to produce anything truthful, Slocum guessed.

Stifling a yawn, Slocum realized he was tired from all the goings-on. He went around the cabin, but Kincannon remained inside, tending to whatever chores, other than searching the women's luggage, he had mentioned earlier. Slocum went to the wagon to fetch his bedroll.

Rachel refused to meet his eye. Maggie looked as though she would explode angrily at any instant. Comfort pouted prettily, but Slocum was not going to make the suggestion that she come with him. That would set off another round of arguing. Of Elizabeth he saw nothing.

"Ladies," he said, tipping his hat and then heading out in search of a quiet place to spread his bedroll. Slocum knew what lay downslope and shivered at the memory of being trapped on the ledge. His footsteps took him in the direction of the outhouse Kincannon had never acknowledged. It was not the best place to sleep, but Slocum figured that somewhere nearby might be better.

The rickety wood house in the sandy pit stank to high heaven, even in the cold mountain air. Slocum hiked past and found an expanse of meadow that had been grassed over earlier in the season but had died back due to the recent freezing nights. The dead grass crinkled under him as he lay down, but the dirt cushioned his body and allowed himself to think he was actually going to get some rest.

Sleep refused to come. Slocum sat up, wondering at what he had seen and had not realized he had seen. He looked around the tiny meadow, then spotted it. Standing, it was easy to miss. At almost ground level, the mound rose up a few inches. Slocum rolled over and got to his feet. He went to the dirt mound and recognized it immediately.

"Fresh grave," he said to himself. He looked around. The outhouse stood in the sandy spit ten yards away. The way station itself was another twenty yards distant. This was a good place for a grave, if you didn't want it noticed by the people on the Mosquito Pass road.

But the mounded dirt was fresh and, unless Slocum missed his guess, the grave was not very deep, as though it had been dug in a powerful hurry. No headstone or cross marked it, and even stones piled atop the dirt to keep coyotes from opening the grave had been overlooked.

He went back to his bedroll, lay down and then wondered if it was all right to go sleep so near a cemetery. Or a fresh grave where the corpse might not have been ready to depart this world quite yet. Slocum rolled onto his side and soon fell asleep, knowing he had more worries than what the Navajos called ghost sickness.

What those worries were, he could not say. And that bothered him most of all.

14

Slocum considered returning to Denver, then looked up into the tall, craggy mountains. Somewhere hidden in the clouds lay Mosquito Pass and, beyond it, Leadville. The appeal of a boomtown drew him now, as much as growing curiosity over the women and their purpose for going to the silver strike at California Gulch outside Leadville. Slocum could make a pile of money in poker games with drunk miners. The women might find their own riches in some wealthy men's beds.

Rachel argued with Kincannon just inside the way station door. Slocum could not overhear what they were so heatedly discussing, but the dark-haired woman stamped her foot, whirled and flounced out as he approached. Slocum hitched the mules and made sure everything was ready for the climb.

Sometime during the night, he had made his decision to see the three women over the Front Range. Why Elizabeth had chosen to stay here was beyond him, but everything about them was a mystery.

"We ought to get rolling," Maggie said, lugging her trunk out. She glared at Slocum when he went to help her. He understood why her luggage was so heavy. If he ever needed to start a war, he knew where to go for the arms. The trunk crashed to the wagon bed, spooking the mules a mite. Rachel already had her carpetbag securely fastened in the wagon.

"Help me, John?" came Comfort's soft, flirty voice. The woman batted her long, dark eyelashes at him and smiled in a way that sent shivers up and down his spine.

"Be glad to," he said, lifting her trunk more easily that the firearms-laden one Maggie had brought out. Slocum knew what was in this trunk. The stacks of letters didn't amount to a whole lot of weight but would complicate the blonde's life when she got over the mountains. Or would it? Slocum suspected that Comfort played the game well, leading on one man and then taking up with another. How many killed each other along the way was something he preferred to stand back and watch rather than get actively caught up in.

"You still have a reward to collect," Comfort said, moving behind him. Her hands stroked over his belly and would have worked lower but Maggie barked at them from the driver's box.

"Get a move on, will you? Time's a' wastin'."

"First time I ever knew her to be in a such a goldanged hurry," muttered Comfort. She gave him one last fond squeeze and then jumped into the wagon bed, her legs dangling over the back edge. The way her skirts hiked up let Slocum see a fair amount of leg.

He forced himself to go around and climb into the box beside Maggie. The redhead fumed, muttering to herself.

Then she snapped, "Get this rig moving."

"Without Rachel?"

"What? Where's that—" She bit off anything more she might have said. Maggie turned and looked toward the cabin. Elizabeth and Kincannon stood nearby, arms around one another.

Slocum had seen lovebirds billing and cooing. Elizabeth and Kincannon stood stiffly, as if they were acting and not doing a good job of it. Elizabeth said something that turned Kincannon red in the face. He started to reply, but Rachel came from the cabin and spoke to both of them. The stationmaster subsided, but his anger continued to boil just under his cheery facade. Slocum was loath to leave because of what the man might do when they were out of sight.

He hoped Elizabeth knew what she was doing. Because he had saved her from Larson, he felt some strange protective urge toward her. He pushed it aside when he remembered how she had paid him in full for rescuing her back in Denver. She was her own woman and could—and would—sleep in whatever bed she made.

"Get in, Rachel. We've got to *go*," Maggie said, begging.

The dark-haired woman silently stalked out and jumped into the back of the wagon next to Comfort. Comfort said something Slocum missed, then shook Rachel's arm as if to wake her from a trance. Rachel jerked back angrily. The two started talking in low tones that Slocum strained to hear. His eavesdropping was ended when the mules began braying. He snapped the reins and got them settled down. He considered using the long whip stuck in a holder beside Maggie, then decided he could keep control with just the reins. When they began a long, steep uphill pull might be the best time to use the whip.

"Gee-haw!" he shouted. The long reins snapped like thunder, and the mules began pulling. Slocum got the wagon onto the road and rattled uphill toward Mosquito Pass. The sun beat down on the back of his neck as it rose over the distant hills to the east, and he saw the reflection of sunlight off snow ahead. All in all, Slocum felt good to be alive and out on the road.

The mood was broken when Maggie bounced against

him as they hit a large rock in the road. She shoved away as though he had burned her.

"Stop it," she said. "Keep this damned wagon from jumping all over creation."

Slocum eased back and let the mules take a brief rest. He faced the woman and said, "This is my wagon, you are my cargo, and if you ever speak to me like that again, you'll find yourself on foot, trying to wrestle your belongings over the pass."

"You wouldn't." Maggie's nostrils flared like a bull about ready to charge. She was hankering for a fight, and Slocum was considering giving it to her. He had taken enough from the women, defending them, keeping their scalps on their heads and their honor intact—almost.

Maggie read the answer in his cold green eyes. She backed off and gripped the edge of the wagon.

"You wouldn't do that to us . . . to three poor women just looking to make a life for themselves."

"Try me."

Slocum was an expert poker player and knew when to bluff, but Maggie was a good enough student of human nature to know there wasn't a speck of bluffing now. He meant what he said.

"I'm sorry, Slocum. I'm under a strain and—"

"Apology accepted," Slocum cut in, not wanting her to go on. He doubted she would tell him anything to ease his curiosity about her and the other women. He snapped the reins again and got the mules pushing hard against their harnesses.

Slocum turned to bark at Maggie for interrupting him again when he saw the red-haired woman had not called out for him to stop, that she was turned around in the seat staring back down the road. He pulled the mules to a halt and twisted around to see Elizabeth waving frantically.

"What's she want?"

"I'll find out," Maggie said, jumping down. Slocum

heaved a sigh and knew it was pointless to rail against cruel fate. He climbed down from the wagon and went to see what Elizabeth had to say. The brunette panted harshly, out of breath from running at this high altitude. Slocum thought it was a good thing she had chosen to stay with the stationmaster. Leadville at an even higher altitude would have kept her winded all the time.

"What's the matter?" he asked. The only reason she would have chased the wagon this far was if something had gone wrong back at the way station. If Kincannon had fallen over the edge of the canyon, Slocum was not about to go back and pick up the battered pieces for a decent burial alongside whoever else had been planted in the shallow grave near the outhouse.

"I changed my mind," Elizabeth said, gasping for air. Her breasts rose and fell, distracting Slocum. She was certainly a lovely woman. The exertion of her run had brought roses to her cheeks and gave her an added beauty that appealed mightily to him.

"About coming?" Maggie asked anxiously.

"Yes, yes," Elizabeth said, getting her wind back. "I can't let you go on. Not after what Rachel said and—" She cut off her explanation when she realized Slocum was listening intently. "Rachel," Elizabeth said, obviously lying now to get him away from what she really meant, "told me what a cad and bounder Walt is. He . . . he hit me when you left."

Slocum said nothing. Women put up with more than that every day on the frontier. It was hard to survive, and a man's nerves snapped now and again. He shook his head. Sometimes it was even harder being a woman out West because of the men. Elizabeth had to have known that when she decided to take up with a man accustomed to such a solitary job.

"Can we get my luggage?" Elizabeth asked.

"Well?" Maggie turned to Slocum, her hands on her

flaring hips. "Are you willing to have another passenger over the pass?"

"Started with four," Slocum said. "No reason to complain about there being four again."

"Thank you, John, thank you," sobbed Elizabeth, clinging to him until Rachel cleared her throat. Elizabeth backed away then and wiped her eyes. "I tried to get my trunk up that first steep hill but didn't quite make it."

Slocum's eyebrows rose. "You got the trunk to the hill? That's a half mile."

"I suppose."

Slocum knew he ought to turn the team around, get back down the hill and load the trunk. But it might be faster if he carried the trunk himself. Harder, but faster.

"Get in the wagon. I'll fetch your trunk."

She lightly kissed him on the cheek to thank him and might have gone farther but Rachel cleared her throat again. Maggie joined in, also, pulling Elizabeth toward the wagon.

"You need to rest, girl," Maggie said loudly. "Let Slocum get your trunk. Then we can be on our way again."

Slocum walked a quarter mile back to where Elizabeth had abandoned her trunk. For a moment, he considered the foolishness of returning without the team, then shrugged it off. It gave him a chance to think about what was swirling around him like some kind of Kansas twister. He grunted as he lifted the trunk to his back and started up the hill. More than giving him a chance to think, it let the women have some time to themselves.

Slocum reckoned there would be a pretty stewpot of emotions in the wagon when he got back. And he was right.

Rachel sat with arms crossed, looking as though she was mad at the world. Comfort blathered on about how good it was having Elizabeth back with them. Maggie and Elizabeth talked, but it didn't look too friendly to Slocum.

He dropped the trunk into the rear of the wagon and wiped the sweat from his forehead. In spite of the cool wind and occasional cloud blocking out the wan heat from the sun, he had struggled getting back.

"Well?" Maggie said, her lips going to a thin line. "Are we standing around or are we traveling?"

She softened her tone a mite when she read Slocum's expression.

"Sorry," she said contritely. Slocum almost believed her. He left the four women in the back of the wagon to thrash out their differences. Hearing what Elizabeth had to say about Kincannon would have suited him just fine, but the brunette had fallen as silent as Rachel.

Slocum got the team straining against the harnesses and back into the twin ruts on the rocky road. He fell into the rhythm of the road, leaning with the motion of the wagon and feeling one with the team, anticipating their problems, doing what he could to make the pulling easier as they headed up another steep incline.

Slocum looked back occasionally to see if the four women were still in the wagon. As crazy as it had gotten, he would not have been surprised to see one or more of them vanish into the rocky countryside. However, they rode along as silent as a grave.

That thought sparked Slocum's memory of where he had spent last night. The grave near the outhouse had been fresh. Then he forgot about it. Men died all the time in the Rockies, from a variety of causes. Some were unnatural, like a bullet to the back, but most were from disease or injury. Any inexperienced traveler along this road would find himself in for a hard time because of the steepness and the increasing altitude. Both Slocum and the mules were gasping when they topped a steep hill and looked out over a relatively level stretch.

Slocum's hand moved toward his holstered six-shooter, then he relaxed.

"What's wrong?" asked Maggie, seeing him move for his gun.

"Can't say yet. There's a stagecoach off the road ahead. Doesn't look to be anyone around it, but it's mighty strange that a driver would abandon such a valuable coach." Slocum had heard some of the Concords went for upward of five thousand dollars. No stage company left that kind of investment sitting beside the road.

"What are we going to do?" Comfort asked nervously. "Are there highwaymen still around?"

"Drive on," Maggie ordered. "Don't stop."

Slocum ignored the redhead and slowed the team until their wagon crept along at a snail's pace. He kept a sharp lookout for trouble. It might be as Comfort feared. Road agents had been known to set up an elaborate trap for unwary travelers, but Slocum didn't think so this time. They rolled along a fairly straight, open stretch of road. If bandits wanted to rob unsuspecting miners on their way to Leadville, they would have given themselves more cover. All he could see were narrow gullies on either side of the road that caught spring runoff or summer showers and carried the water downhill.

Not much of a hiding place for masked men to jump from, with six-shooters waving in the air.

"Slocum!" cried Maggie. "Don't stop. This is a trap of some kind."

"Hello!" Slocum called, reining in and stopping the wagon a dozen feet from the stagecoach. It tilted at a crazy angle, leading Slocum to believe the rear axle had broken. The team was gone, as were any passengers and their baggage. It was as though the stage had broken down and everyone aboard simply vanished.

"Who's that? That you, Edgar?" A shaggy head poked up from inside the stage. The man opened the door and stepped out, blinking at the sunlight. When he focused on

Slocum, he spat and wiped his lips. "T'aint you, is it, Edgar? Who might you be?"

"Name's Slocum. What happened?" Behind him, Slocum heard Maggie start to open her trunk. He wanted to warn her not to open fire but held his tongue. If he showed he knew she carried an arsenal, there'd be a passel of questions to answer.

"I'm the driver for this woebegone rig," the man said, jumping down. From the way he limped over to stand beside Slocum, he had been injured.

"You need help?"

"You mean 'cuz of the way I hobble about? Naw. Nuthin' nobody kin do 'bout that. Name's Frosty. They call me that 'cuz I got frostbit toes in the winter of '72 and had to chop 'em off."

"What about the stagecoach?" Slocum heard Maggie's trunk lid close. She seemed to be taking a wait-and-see attitude toward Frosty and his plight.

"That's my coach. Well, I drive it for the Denver Stage Line. We was comin' along hell fer leather—'scuse the French, ladies—and I hit this rock. Busted the damn axle. Must be four days ago now."

"You had passengers?" asked Elizabeth.

"Shore did, little lady. Got them on to the next way station, then I hiked back to wait fer help. Company's not gonna like havin' to fix this one up. Brand-new coach from back East."

Slocum saw that this much was true. There were only a few scrapes on the coach's sides and no bullet holes.

"Edgar's supposed to come help?" asked Slocum.

"You know him? A real pistol, that Edgar. Why, there was this time when we—"

"I don't know him," Slocum cut in, not wanting a re-telling of every barroom fight and drunken binge Frosty had ever been on. "If you leave it canted like that, the damage'll get worse if the stagecoach shifts."

"Don't I know it," Frosty said, running his gnarled hand through a mat of filthy, unkempt hair. "Cain't do nuthin' about it by myself."

"If we can get a log long enough to lever up the coach, we can take some weight off those rawhide springs," Slocum said.

"No, you can't. We've been delayed enough," Maggie protested. "You said so yourself, Slocum. Winter storms. Snow. We might be caught and have to go back to Denver."

"Lady's right on that score," Frosty said. "Every minute counts this time o' year, but I'd surely appreciate any help you can give. Might even be a few bucks in it from the company fer savin' their valuable property."

"Pitch camp," Slocum said, eyeing the sun grazing the mountains ahead. It got dark fast on this side of the Front Range, and by the time he'd hoist the stagecoach onto a block, it would be dark.

"You don't know what this means to me, Slocum," Frosty said. He grinned, showing a gold front tooth. "Been out her for two days all by my lonesome and now I git a real friend comin' to my aid, not to mention seein' four lovely ladies. A shame you ladies didn't take my coach. I'd've treated you right."

Comfort smiled and said, "Why, you're such a gentleman, Mr. Frosty. Thank you. I—"

"Comfort," Maggie said, glancing from the blonde to Rachel, who only glared. "Slocum said to get camp set up. Let's do it while he helps out this, uh, this unfortunate man."

Slocum and Frosty scoured the countryside until they found a limb strong enough and long enough to make a difference. While Slocum used the limb to lever up the coach, Frosty shoved rocks under the back until the stagecoach sat level.

"Might jist have saved havin' to replace both back

wheels, too," Frosty said, admiring their handiwork. "I'll put in a word for you with the Leadville office."

"Thanks," Slocum said. "Does the Denver Stage Company keep an office open all year long in Leadville?"

"Sorta. One agent there. Mostly does what he can to find jobs for the stationmasters along this road."

Slocum pursued his lips, then asked, "How long since you hit Kincannon's way station?"

"Who? Don't know the name."

Slocum described Walter Kincannon, adding in way of explanation, "The stationmaster at the last cabin back along the road."

"Kincannon? Naw, that ain't his name. That's Slattery. Don't know no other name. Slattery's been with the company goin' on four years, almost as long as I've driven for 'em."

"Maybe I got the name wrong," Slocum said.

"The way you described him ain't Slattery, neither. Slattery's 'bout my height, only shorter. And uglier. Got three-four scars on his face makin' it look like a checkerboard, and the way he hobbles along on his gimpy leg makes me look like a frisky thoroughbred horse trottin' out to stud."

"You join us for some dinner?" Slocum invited. "The ladies aren't much when it comes to cooking, but they are a real sight for sore eyes."

"Never seen purtier," Frosty agreed. "And I kin help along things a mite. I brung a pint or two with me to while away the time. Think them ladies would care for a snort?"

"Never hurts to ask," Slocum said, wondering what kind of reception the offer would get.

Comfort was the only one to take Frosty up on the offer of whiskey. Slocum wondered how much farther things might go with the two, then decided he did not care. He spread his bedroll under the wagon bed and tried to go to sleep. What Frosty had told him about the stationmaster at the last stop worried him. Still, the stage driver had been there more than five days back and things might have changed. The company could have replaced Slattery in that time.

Slocum's musings were disturbed when he saw a dark shape moving away from the camp. He pushed back the blanket and shivered at the cold, got on his boots and followed at a distance. This might be an innocent trip to answer a call of nature, but Slocum didn't want any more problems like Comfort falling over a cliff to slow them.

In darkness made even more intense by clouds rolling down from the upper elevations, Slocum could not identify the woman he followed. Then he stopped and relied more on hearing. A second shape, taller, more ruggedly built rose from the shadows.

Slocum knew answers to a lot of his questions might be at hand. As he moved closer to get a good look at both the man and the woman, he froze in his tracks. Something wasn't right. Then boots on gravel behind him gave him scant warning before something very heavy crashed into his skull.

The darkness turned complete as he crashed to the ground, unconscious.

15

Stars mixed with rocks as Slocum was dragged along by his heels. He jerked to keep his face from banging into a large stone and found himself rolling over again, this time sliding along the ground on his back and staring at the sky. Clouds moved slowly to hide the stars again, plunging the mountains into utter blackness.

At the thought of such darkness, Slocum winced. The lump on the back of his head began to throb. Memories were slowly returning. He had followed someone from camp. Who? He didn't know, but Slocum was sure that the woman had met a man. Before he had gotten close enough to see what was happening, the boom was lowered on the back of his head.

And now? Slocum tried to kick free, only to find that his ankles were securely roped together. He was flipped over again and dragged up a steep slope facedown.

The pain from a dozen cuts on his face was nothing compared to the jolts of agony inside his head. Whoever had slugged him had not been gentle—and being pulled up the hill was taking its toll on him, too. Pain hit him from every direction, unexpectedly striking a rib, moving to his knees, going back to his skull as he was twisted around again.

But now Slocum heard grunts and puffing, as if someone was exerting himself in the thin mountain air. Slocum tried to relax and hoard his strength for the best moment to get free. Whoever had hit him had yet to realize he had regained consciousness.

A final grunt and he was thrown flat on his belly. Slocum lay still, tensing and relaxing muscles to give him a better idea what he could and could not do. Whoever had hit him from behind had left him his six-shooter. Good. What wasn't as good, the leather thong over the hammer to keep the six-gun from bouncing from his holster was still in place. He could not remove the keeper without betraying himself.

His eyes flickering open, Slocum tried to make out his attacker. No one was in sight, meaning that the man was on Slocum's other side. Trying to pull his feet apart told him he was still hog-tied. With his feet roped together, he didn't stand much chance in a fight.

Unless he got to his six-shooter.

"You sure are a heavy galoot to look so puny."

The words shocked Slocum. He recognized Bear Zacharias's voice immediately.

Then he was sailing through the air. The bounty hunter had picked him up and tossed him aside as easily as if he had been a sack of potatoes. Slocum hit the ground hard, jolted and in excruciating pain.

His groan alerted Zacharias that his prisoner was back among the living.

"You little skunk," Zacharias said, picking up Slocum and hanging him upside down from a tree limb. Slocum swung to and fro in the wind, his head barely an inch off the ground. "You done left me for them Injuns to kill."

"H-how'd you get away?" Slocum's hands were free, for all the good it did him. He reached down—above his head—to stop swinging. He no longer swayed like a pendulum in a Regulator clock, but he could not see Zacharias, either. The bounty hunter remained behind him.

Slocum glanced down and saw his Colt Navy was still in its holster, but he dared not make a grab for it. His hands were cut up and bloody from being dragged into Zacharias's camp. If he drew the six-shooter and it slipped from his grip, he was a goner. Better to bide his time, get the six-shooter out and fire it when it would do the most good—and when he could see the bounty hunter.

"No thanks to you," Zacharias said. Slocum heard the bounty hunter pacing but caught only glimpses of his scuffed boots inches from his head. "I waltzed on into that Injun camp purty as you please, wantin' to find me a pretty li'l blonde lady with a price on her head. I almost got my scalp lifted for my trouble!"

Slocum couldn't figure out how much bounty money rode on Comfort's head for Zacharias to be this persistent. He thought the bounty hunter had exaggerated when he had claimed a thousand dollars. Most men would chuck it after fighting off an entire band of Arapahos unless it was a sizable amount.

A cold shiver went up and down Slocum's spine. Was that why the Arapahos had not come after him and Rachel? Had Zacharias killed all the Indians? It didn't seem possible, but it explained a whale of a lot.

"They shot me up good, you no-account cur," Zacharias ranted on. "Four arrows and a bullet! And when I got to lookin' for the blonde, she wasn't there. Gone. You snuck her out, didn't you, you li'l weasel?"

"No, no, she wasn't there," Slocum said. "She went back to Denver. She knew you were onto her and—"

He gasped when Zacharias started using him for a punching bag as expertly as Gentleman Jim Corbett might. Slocum tightened his belly and took the blows. He eyed his six-gun again, but his hands still ached. There was no way in hell he could use that six-shooter with his usual expertise, especially not hanging upside down.

"You lyin' sack o' shit," Zacharias growled. "It was damned lucky I happened on you out there. Might have missed you entirely."

Slocum's vision doubled as pain worked its way throughout his body. He was only half aware of what was happening when Zacharias stopped punishing him with his hamlike fists and stepped back, panting harshly.

"This ain't gettin' me nowhere," the bounty hunter declared. "If you're here, that means the blonde is, too."

"No," Slocum grated out, trying to argue with Zacharias. The word came out as a weak mewling and, for a moment, Slocum blacked out. When he came to, he had the feeling that not much time had passed. But could he be sure?

He reached up and tried to grab his ankles and pull himself up enough to get the ropes off his ankles. He was too weak. Flopping back, Slocum began swinging like a pendulum and finally grabbed a nearby bush. With supreme effort, he pulled harder and harder until his back arched and he thought he would break it.

When he couldn't take it any longer, he let go and swung fast toward the tree. He crashed into it, arms outstretched and grabbing for it like a long-lost lover. Hanging on, he began working his way up the trunk with excruciating slowness. His body screamed in pain, but he ignored it. Bear Zacharias had set off for the women's camp. If he got there, he'd try to take Comfort into custody—and Maggie, with her arsenal, was not likely to allow that.

Slocum wanted to avoid bloodshed. Except for the bounty hunter's blood, and he wanted to be responsible for spilling that personally.

A low limb on the juniper allowed Slocum to work his way almost upright. He threw his arms around the limb and inched his way down to where Zacharias had knotted the rope to the limb. He untied the knot and fell to the ground, panting with the exertion. Slocum tried to stand but his legs were too weak. Instead of pushing himself to impossible limits, he sat with his back against the tree trunk for a few minutes and marshaled his strength.

"Got to get back," he told himself grimly, once the numbness had gone and he knew he could endure the pain in his belly and back. Forcing himself to his feet, he took a few tottering steps, then strengthened. When he was sure he wasn't going to collapse, he did what he could to clean the blood and dirt off his hands and then slipped the leather thong off the hammer of his Colt.

He was ready for Bear.

Slocum scouted around, hunting for footprints that showed the direction Zacharias had gone. It took Slocum a few precious minutes to locate the bounty hunter's trail, but then he went as quickly as he could through the dark night. Anxiety grew as he hurried along, knowing that Zacharias was not likely to leave Maggie alive if she went for any of the guns in her trunk. And what if it came down to a shootout between the bounty hunter and Rachel? Slocum was not sure which of that pair was the most vicious. The memory of Rachel cutting down Larson and enjoying the man's death haunted him.

It might be worth letting Zacharias blunder into the camp if Rachel was ready for him. Slocum had no love for the bounty hunter, but he doubted if Rachel would have a pistol cocked and aimed. Zacharias would take them by surprise if they were not expecting anyone but Slocum to return.

Or would one of the women at the wagon expect someone else? Who had sneaked off to talk to the man in the night? Slocum had not been able to identify either the man or woman before Zacharias had slugged him.

As he rushed along, he got the feeling someone was ahead. He knew it might be the stagecoach driver, and he did not want to plug him by mistake. Slocum slowed, then crept forward, his Colt Navy out and ready to put a slug in the bounty hunter's worthless, rock-hard gut, if Zacharias waited for him.

He lifted his six-shooter and sighted, then lowered the gun when he realized it wasn't the bounty hunter sitting on the rock. Slocum inched ahead, then, *sotto voce*, said, "That you, Elizabeth?"

The huddled dark figure jerked about, her hand going to her throat. A small silver moonbeam illuminated the side of the woman's face. He had identified her accurately.

"John?"

"You see Zacharias go by here?"

"The bounty hunter? I haven't seen anyone. I . . . I came out here to be alone, to think."

"About Kincannon?" There was a lot Slocum could not figure out, but it had to wait until after he finished off Bear Zacharias. He had a big score to settle with the man and wasn't going to be distracted until the bounty hunter was squarely in his sights and had a bullet in his head.

"Well, yes, among other things. I'm not sure I did right. I—"

"There's no time. Zacharias is hunting for Comfort and knows she's somewhere near." Slocum tried to get his bearings. The disabled stagecoach, Frosty, the wagon and the rest of the women looked to be ahead, in the direction of Zacharias's tracks. He might beat the man to the wagon if he cut up and over the hill behind Elizabeth.

"Who is he, John? Why is he after us?"

Slocum hesitated, thinking that over. Zacharias was not the kind of man to go after nickel-and-dime rewards. Whatever had been offered for Comfort's return had to be huge. For all that, Larson and Kincannon were probably in it for the money, too. But what money? There had to be a pile of gold waiting for the right man to claim. Somehow, the four women held the key to it.

"You know why, Elizabeth," Slocum said, taking a shot. "It's not just Comfort he's after, is it? He wants you, too."

"What!"

Slocum tried to get a better look at the woman's face. The brunette had to be a better actress than he gave her credit for to seem so astounded at the notion that Zacharias was after her, too.

"You know why," Slocum went on relentlessly. "You and Comfort. And Maggie and Rachel, too."

"There's no way he could—" Elizabeth clamped her mouth shut. Now she looked defiant, as if challenging Slocum to torture the information out of her.

"Larson's dead. What about Kincannon?"

"Why should he be dead? I left him back at the way station."

"He's not the stationmaster, is he? A man named Slattery is—or was. I think his grave was by the outhouse. When I first arrived, Kincannon sent me away from the outhouse so I wouldn't see the fresh grave. He killed Slattery, didn't he?"

"Oh, John, he's such an evil man! He's capable of anything. He told me the real stationmaster had gone and that he'd hurt me if I said anything, if I didn't stay with him."

Slocum began to get antsy. Zacharias was not taking time to unravel small mysteries when he had a big reward to collect if he bagged Comfort.

"We've got to get back to warn the others," Slocum said. "Did you get here from over that hill?" He pointed to the one behind Elizabeth. She nodded numbly.

Again, he wondered if she was a good actress or if she really was upset over Kincannon and the notion that he might have gunned down the stationmaster before they arrived. That set Slocum thinking in other directions. For Kincannon to kill Slattery, he had to arrive ahead of them—and had to know they were on the way. But why kill the stationmaster and then impersonate him? Travelers along the road stopped over all the time. Kincannon could have pretended to be on his way to Leadville while waiting for Elizabeth and the others to reach the station.

Slocum had too much to think about. He wished he could have dropped to a cold rock beside Elizabeth and think it all through, but there was a time for thinking and a time for acting. He had to act if he wanted to stop Zacharias.

Without waiting to see if Elizabeth followed, he began trudging up the hill. Slocum had a basic idea of the lay of the land. This more direct route ought to bring him out onto the road over Mosquito Pass but in front of the wagon. Zacharias would arrive from behind. Taking the bounty hunter by surprise looked like Slocum's best plan.

As he reached the road, Elizabeth called out from higher on the hill.

"John, wait for me. Please. We need to talk!"

He cursed under his breath. He doubted that her voice carried far enough along the road to warn Zacharias, but this was a life-and-death contest. Any advantage he lost, no matter how small, might mean the difference between taking out Zacharias and ending up swinging like a pendulum from a tree limb, once more the bounty hunter's prisoner.

"Quiet," he ordered. The woman stumbled over to him, breathless from chasing him. Elizabeth clung to his arm for a moment, her weight unbalancing him. He jerked free so his gun hand was away from her. Slocum looked down the road toward the wagon but saw no one. A small campfire guttered to coals a few yards away, but he didn't see anyone there. The abandoned stagecoach stood silently a dozen yards farther east, but he saw no trace of the driver.

"I'm sorry, John. I know this is serious, but I want to help. Tell me what to do."

"Stay here and shut up," he snapped. This shocked the woman. She recoiled and stared at him with wide brown eyes. Then anger caused her lips to thin to a line.

"Very well," she said. "If that's the way you feel about me."

Slocum knew that arguing with Elizabeth was futile. She might not understand how relentless Zacharias could be—or how brutal. This was a man who had killed off most of an Arapaho hunting party. Cats were supposed to have nine lives. The bounty hunter had already outlived any cat.

Slocum wanted to pump enough bullets into Zacharias so he could erase whatever number of lives the bounty hunter had remaining.

A sharp crack caused Slocum to go into a gunfighter's crouch, his Colt aimed in the direction of the campfire where the report had come from. No sign of a gunman. Slocum advanced carefully, not wanting to blunder into a trap. Another shot echoed up the road, followed by angry shouts.

He could not make out the words, but the pitch was high enough to convince him that the women were in trouble. Another shot and another, then Slocum was running pell-mell for the wagon. He ducked behind one wheel and peered around the wagon bed, his six-gun ready for action.

The fire crackled and popped, sending tiny sparks twisting into the cold Colorado night. Other than this movement, he saw nothing. The shouts and shots had come from the direction where Zacharias would have entered the camp.

As nervous as a prostitute in church, Slocum walked to the fire and looked around for any trace of the women or the bounty hunter.

Nothing.

He cocked his head to one side and listened hard. The echoes had died down. He heard nothing unusual in the nighttime. Slocum had arrived too late. The women had vanished, along with Bear Zacharias.

16

Slocum spun when he heard movement behind him. He had to check himself to keep from shooting Elizabeth. The woman had come up, frightened and looking around wildly.

"Where are they?" she cried. "What happened to them?"

"Can't say," Slocum said. "Reckon Zacharias might have them." He tried to find tracks on the rocky ground, but it was so scuffled up he could not identify individual footprints. He got a notion of the direction the women went, but not why—unless someone had forced them at gunpoint.

"I can't stand it any more," Elizabeth said, shivering. She turned away. Her shoulders trembled as she sobbed bitterly. "This is all too much for me!"

She began shaking as though she had the grippe. Slocum scooped up his bedroll from the wagon and draped the blanket around her. Elizabeth turned toward him, buried her face in his shoulder and cried uncontrollably. He held her awkwardly, considering what lay ahead of him. None of it held much appeal.

Tracking in the dark was dangerous. Zacharias could

lay an ambush for him. Slocum would be dead before he knew there was any problem lurking around him. And, as good as he was, following where the women had been taken might be impossible in the dark. If he lost the trail, he might wander in the wrong direction, dooming them by never finding them at all. A single mistake meant someone's death, his or theirs.

Slocum thought hard on this, deciding not to go after Zacharias and his prisoners until sunup. If Zacharias had not killed them outright, he might not kill them at all. The women might give the mountain of a man some pleasure—and each one of the trio might have rewards on their pretty heads. If so, Zacharias would keep them alive.

Unless the rewards were offered "dead or alive." The bounty hunter was as likely to have his way with them, then kill them. A dead criminal would not accuse him of rape.

Slocum was in the dark in more than one way. He held Elizabeth tightly as he studied the sky. From the fast-moving clouds, a storm would hit within the hour. Any tracks would be erased if he did not move quickly, but to do so might mean his own death.

"Go after them, John, please, please," sobbed Elizabeth.

"If Zacharias kills me, your friends are dead, too," Slocum told her. "I've got to be smarter than him." Slocum wondered how Zacharias had done as well as he had, charging about like a bull in a china shop. Bullets and arrows meant little to the huge bounty hunter. Slocum had already seen that being knocked over a cliff had not done the man in.

Slocum smiled crookedly. He had taken his share of punishment and was still alive. And hadn't he been trapped on the ledge and lived to talk about it? True, he had been rescued, but he had survived. He was smarter than Zacharias—and as tough.

"You have to be safe first," Slocum said, turning her

away from the camp and heading to the far side of the road. It was colder now, the wind picking up. He thought he saw a cave a hundred yards away. Elizabeth could hide there while he went after the bounty hunter.

"I don't want to be alone," she said, "but I want you to save Rachel, Maggie and Comfort. Oh, John, I'm so confused!"

They went into the cave, which turned out to be hardly more than a deep depression in the rocky hill. It was adequate for blocking the cuttingly cold wind and gave protection from observation. Slocum doubted that Zacharias wanted to make a clean sweep of the women. He would be happy with Comfort and the other two. It still took a load off Slocum's conscience knowing Elizabeth would be safe.

He had to admit, to himself if not to the woman, that he might not find Zacharias in time. With the storm coming up, he might not find the bounty hunter at all.

Elizabeth clung to him as he spread out his heavy blanket and sat on it beside her. Her crying had stopped, but she sniffled a little now and then.

"You must think me a terrible baby," she said, turning her teary brown eyes up to look at him.

"You've been through a lot," he said. "It's not every week you get kidnapped and shot at and . . . see your husband again. You and Kincannon never got a divorce, did you?"

"How'd you know?" She pushed back from him. "How'd you know we were married?"

"A guess," Slocum said. "There's no way a smart, beautiful, determined woman like you is going to take up with a man she just met unless there was a history. If he was only a boyfriend, I don't reckon you would have stayed like you did. From what I could see, you weren't feeling much but fear, after the surprise at seeing him wore off."

"You don't miss much, do you, John?" Elizabeth snuggled closer. He should have pushed her away. Elizabeth was a married woman. But he didn't. Slocum remembered what it had been like with her when he had rescued her from Larson.

For a spell they said nothing. In a small voice Elizabeth finally said, "You can't know what it was like being with him. He was horrible. When Maggie and the others came through Denver, I saw my chance to get away and start over."

"By marrying a man in Leadville?" He remembered the letters in her trunk.

"Something like that. But I don't want to talk about it. Not right now." She moved even closer, her firm breasts rubbing against him. He had qualms about what he and Elizabeth had done before, after he had saved her from Larson. Now that he knew she was still married, he knew it wasn't right.

But it felt right. Slocum kissed her. Elizabeth returned the kiss with more passion than he had thought possible to be locked up inside her. Her mouth eagerly devoured his, and her tongue came slipping forth to erotically duel with his. He held her tightly in his arms as they kissed deeply, then sank back onto the blanket he had spread on the dusty cave floor.

The wind howled louder outside, but all that Slocum heard were Elizabeth's tiny moans of desire. Desire for him. His hands began roaming her lush body, finding all the right places to give her even more pleasure.

He pressed into one breast through the layers of her thick clothing. In spite of the thick cloth, he felt the fleshy nub of her nipple begin to harden. It turned into a taut button of lust that pulsed with every beat of her excited heart. He pinched down harder on that nipple, and Elizabeth melted against him.

"Yes, John, so nice, so very nice. But I want more."

She thrust her hand down against his crotch. Nimble fingers unbuttoned his fly and released his erect manhood. Slocum gasped with relief as his rigid organ escaped the denim prison and was immediately caught by Elizabeth's grasping, warm hand.

She stroked gently up and down until he thought he might explode like a stick of dynamite. She sensed his arousal and moved away, no longer devoting as much attention to his length with her hand. Instead, she slid down his body and kissed the very tip of his erection.

Slocum shuddered with the intensity of the feelings in his loins. His balls tightened, forcing him to exert all his self-control to keep from acting like some kid getting his first piece of tail. He tried to tell Elizabeth to slow down, but she was too hot for that. Her ruby lips clamped firmly on the tip of his shaft.

She bobbed up and down, taking more and more of him into her sucking mouth with every movement. Slocum worked to get his gun belt free while she tended to his manhood so expertly.

"More?" she asked, teasing him. Elizabeth looked up, her brown eyes gleaming. Her pink tongue snaked out and raked along the underside of his erection, causing a shudder to pass from toes to the top of his head.

"That answer your silly question?" he said. Slocum half sat up and worked at the buttons on Elizabeth's blouse. Her milky white globes popped out. He saw the coppery plains around her rigid nipples and thought of a bull's-eye. Using both hands he manhandled her breasts, being sure to catch the nipples between thumb and forefinger and roll those delightful nips around.

Elizabeth could no longer hold him in her mouth. She was moaning in pleasure and beginning to thrash about. Reaching down, she pulled up her skirts and began rubbing between her legs.

"That's my job," Slocum said, using his twin handholds

to scoot her up next to him on the blanket. She rolled onto her back, her legs drifting apart to reveal the furry triangle nestled between her creamy thighs. Tiny dewdrops of moisture sparkled there, telling him she was ready for him.

But Slocum was not going to rush this. She had tormented him and he wanted to return the favor—and the pleasure. Bending low, he kissed the insides of her thighs, dragging his wet tongue along until he almost reached the fragrant tangled nest hiding her nether lips. He moved one hand down lower and inserted a wiggling finger deep into her most intimate recess.

Elizabeth arched her back and ground her crotch down into his hand, groaning with intense pleasure. She mumbled something over and over but Slocum could not make it out. And he did not care. He was too involved in giving her all the ecstasy she could handle.

Running his finger in and out of her oily gash excited the brunette, but it also excited Slocum to the point where he could hardly stand it any longer. He rolled over between the woman's wantonly widespread legs and moved up to where his engorged organ bumped into the well-lubricated nether lips his finger parted.

"Now, John, hurry. Fast. Hard, I need it, oh!"

Elizabeth gasped when Slocum levered his hips forward and sank all the way into her steamy interior. One moment he was out in the cold night air. The next he was surrounded by clingingly hot female flesh. When Elizabeth arched her back and began moving her hips, he thought he would lose all control. He fought back the fiery tide building within him and worked his hips in a circle opposite to the way Elizabeth moved.

This ground their groins together in such a powerfully sensuous mix that Slocum lost all power over himself.

He pulled back and then slammed forward with all the passion hidden away inside him. He felt the woman's body respond instantly. The inner sheath of female flesh clamped down hard, trying to keep him inside her. He raced back, the heat of friction burning away at him. Without knowing it, he began moving faster, driving deeper, lifting her off the ground.

Elizabeth gasped with every insertion. And Slocum floated away as the emotions mounted within him and the physical needs took total control of his actions.

He was distantly aware of her clawing at his back as orgasm crushed her tender body. Slocum worked faster, his hips like they were driving a mechanical piston. The heat burned along his entire length, and the white-hot tide in the steam boiler of his balls finally erupted. He arched his back and tried to split her body apart with his fleshy sword.

Elizabeth cried out in release again, clinging fiercely to him. They moved together and then Slocum sank down, sweating and drained. Elizabeth moved closer and threw one bare leg over his hips. He wasn't going anywhere, even if he wanted to.

"Oh," she said in a little girl voice belying the very womanly lovemaking they had just engaged in. "It's turning all limp inside me."

"About the way I feel all over," Slocum allowed. "You plumb wore me out."

"Not forever, I hope," Elizabeth said, nuzzling at his neck. Her hot breath and wet tongue worked on him. Slocum knew he shouldn't stay with her, not like this, but he gave in to his desires.

They kissed and fondled each other, but it was Elizabeth who pushed him away when he started getting intimately interested again and could do something about it.

"What's wrong?" he asked.

"Maggie, Rachel, Comfort," she said. "It's not right letting them be taken off like that. Isn't there anything you can do? Anything at all? I'd be mighty grateful. Again."

She thrust her tongue into his ear and rolled it about before moving back to hear his answer.

Slocum thought on the matter. It wasn't right being with a married woman like this, even if she had left her husband. He told himself that Elizabeth had intended on marrying another man in Leadville, probably without getting a divorce from Kincannon—or telling her new groom. And he knew none of the women were too shy about sharing their favors with anyone who caught their fancy.

But it wasn't right. And it wasn't right he should enjoy this lovemaking while the other women were in Zacharias's clutches. The bounty hunter probably had not gone far. Back to his camp was a good guess, and Slocum knew he could find it again, even in the moonless dark and burgeoning storm. The bounty hunter wouldn't be happy that Slocum had escaped but might not be looking for him to return so soon.

"I'll go after them," Slocum said. The wind whined through rocks, and tiny snow pellets danced about on the gusts. He had feared a mountain storm since leaving Denver, and his fears were being realized. If he didn't get to the other women fast, he might not be able to rescue them at all.

"Let me help you," Elizabeth offered, buttoning his jeans. The way she did it sent tremors of desire into Slocum again. When he buckled on his gun belt once more, he was well nigh as uncomfortable as he had been before Elizabeth had released him earlier.

But the biting cold took care of a second erection the instant he stepped into the wind. Slocum pulled up his collar and held his arms close to his body. Holding on to his hat, he headed back to the wagon to find Zacharias's path and free the women.

The fire had gone out completely while he and Elizabeth had dallied. Slocum got his bearings, then started off in the direction of Zacharias's camp. Slocum stumbled over something on the ground. He turned colder when he saw it was the stage driver. Frosty had been plugged smack between the eyes and now had a thin layer of snow all over him.

Slocum's resolve firmed as he realized he had to stop Zacharias once and for all. His long strides covered the distance in half the time it had taken the bounty hunter to drag him there. When Slocum whipped out his six-shooter and swung it around the camp, ready to plug Zacharias, he found only empty space.

There was no trace of the women or Zacharias. Moreover, Slocum could not see that the bounty hunter had even returned to the camp.

Slocum hurried back to the wagon, found the dead campfire, then retraced the path taken by the women, alert now for other spoor. His sharp eyes saw a shiny brass cartridge. Picking it up and examining it, Slocum saw it was a spent .44. Zacharias hadn't carried a rifle and had carried a shotgun during the attack on the Arapaho camp.

Taking a guess as to direction, Slocum headed out into the night without any clear destination. The women's tracks were long gone under a dusting of snow, and he followed more on faith than skill. Rocks rose and steep inclines dictated where they most likely had been herded along. If they had fought off their attacker, a body would have been evident long since.

The vivid memory of Rachel gunning down Larson kept returning to haunt Slocum. The woman was no stranger to killing. If Rachel had a six-gun, she would have used it without a qualm. Not seeing Zacharias's corpse told him the women were captives. Again.

He skidded and slipped on the steep decline, the dark and the storm clutching at him like groping hands. Slocum grabbed on to a rock and stopped himself from taking a fall when he saw an abrupt bluff suddenly appear in front of him. Panting harshly, he regained his wits. A game trail ran along the edge of the precipice. Here and there he saw places where stones had been kicked, revealing fresh dirt not yet blown away by the strong wind or covered with snow.

"Been here recently," he said to himself. Slocum made sure his six-shooter slid free in his holster, then walked along the game trail until he saw a fire blazing merrily ahead. Shouts fought against the wind, but Slocum recognized Maggie's voice.

He hurried along, ready for trouble.

Comfort and Rachel were tied together near the fire. Maggie held a rock and swung it clumsily as Kincannon tried to grab her.

"Don't be like that, li'l lady," he said mockingly. "I'll show you something hard, something hard and warm that'll positively tickle yer fancy."

"You son of a bitch," Maggie snarled. She lunged at him, trying to brain him with the sharp rock. Her foot went out from under her on a snowy patch, and she fell heavily. Kincannon swarmed over her, pinning her hands by gripping her wrists. He shifted so his knees pressed into her shoulders. Try as she might, Maggie could not get the heavier man off her.

"Now, you're gonna enjoy this, maybe as much as I will." He held both of her wrists in one hand and moved to unbutton his fly.

"Might be," Slocum said, "but you're not going to like it as much as I am."

"Slocum!"

Kincannon kicked away from Maggie and clumsily went for his gun. Slocum was faster. His first bullet struck Kincannon squarely in the the chest. Before the man had time to realize he was dead, Slocum got off another round. This slug ripped through the fake station master's forehead, matching the one that had killed Frosty.

"Damn you, Slocum!" shouted Maggie. "I wanted to kill him myself!"

To this Slocum had no response. He stared at Kincannon's corpse, wondering if he had killed the man because he had just screwed his wife and this put things right, or if it was only justice for Kincannon killing Slattery and Frosty.

It didn't much matter, he decided. Those two bullets had righted more than one wrong.

"The storm's going to be on us if we don't shake a leg and get back to the wagon," Slocum told the women. Maggie had already freed both Rachel and Comfort. Rachel glared at him, and Slocum knew he could repeat what he and Elizabeth had done earlier with Comfort from her adoring look.

He started back along the trail without giving any of them a chance to say a word. He wasn't up to verbal abuse or more physical pleasure right then.

17

The snow started with only windblown hard pellets the size of buckshot, then turned to larger wet flakes that melted the instant they hit Slocum's face. He wiped the dampness off before it froze with every new gust of wind tearing at his skin. Pulling his coat around him no longer helped. He shivered as he lost heat faster than his body could generate it.

The notion of snuggling up next to Comfort under a blanket appealed to him more and more. If they had a blanket.

Rachel and Maggie trailed behind, in spite of his continued commands for them to stay close. Getting separated if the snow worsened would be sure death.

Sure death. The words rattled around in Slocum's head like pebbles in a can. It had been sure death for Larson to kidnap Elizabeth. And it had been sure death for Kincannon to kidnap the other three women. The pattern developing did not please Slocum one bit. One—or all four—got into trouble and he ended up getting them out of it, after someone died at his hand.

Walt Kincannon's death did not bother Slocum, though. He was sure the man had killed Slattery back at the way station and was probably guilty of more than that, besides Frosty's death. His treatment of Elizabeth had also been less than civilized. Slocum saw nothing to mourn in the man's sudden demise. But how many other surprises could the four women pop up with before they reached Leadville?

If they reached the boomtown.

New snow blinded Slocum for a moment. He blinked it out of his eyes and squinted. The trail was covered by a half inch of freshly-blown snow, forcing him to find the way back to the wagon by instinct. As he trudged along, boots crunching in the snow and the wind's whistle filling his ears, he worried about the bounty hunter. Bear Zacharias had vanished off the face of the earth again.

But every time he did, he showed up when it was most inconvenient. Slocum owed him big time and intended to deliver when their paths crossed again, as he knew they would. Bear Zacharias was like a bad penny that kept returning. Slocum just hoped it would be later rather than sooner when he found the bounty hunter, because the storm promised to give him more trouble than he could handle over the next few hours.

"Can we get back to the way station?" asked Comfort. She hurried to keep up with his long, ground-devouring strides. Slocum wondered if he walked this fast to stay warm or to keep away from the blonde and the other two. Maybe it was a little of both since the storm and the women meant trouble for him.

"I doubt it," he said. "We used up most of the food when we were there, and I didn't see any firewood nearby. Our best chance is to ride out the storm on the road."

"What about the stagecoach driver back there?" Comfort jerked her thumb over her shoulder, indicating the road toward the way station where Slocum had helped Frosty. From the way his own toes felt at the moment,

Slocum hoped he wouldn't join the stage driver in losing his toes to frostbite.

"Kincannon killed him," Slocum said. "He expected help any time, but I don't think we ought to rely on Edgar showing up to save us."

"It doesn't seem right, leaving such a nice man out there without burying him," Comfort said almost wistfully.

"What's not going to be right is us freezing to death," Slocum said. He dropped to one knee and brushed away the snow on the ground. He swept an even larger patch clear as Rachel and Maggie came up, their breath erupting from their noses like fire-breathing dragons.

"What is it, John?" Comfort asked.

"You thinking to dig to China?" asked Maggie. "You better dig fast, because I'm freezing."

"The road," Slocum said. "I wanted to be sure I'd found it." He looked in both directions, then decided uphill was the best bet for finding the wagon and mules. The mules had to be moved out of the wind or they would die quickly. And if the mules did, so would they.

"Well, hurray for our scout," Rachel said sarcastically. "He found the road." She quieted when a new blast of frigid wind caused her to suck in her breath. If she had taken a look at the ground, she would have seen how difficult it was even finding the road. The snow drifted fast, covering the road up to an inch in places—and the storm was just beginning.

Less than a ten-minute hike brought them to the wagon. Slocum now had to shout over the howling wind.

"Get all the blankets and what clothing you can use to stay warm. We're heading that way," he said, pointing in the direction of the cave where he had left Elizabeth. "Get something for Elizabeth, will you?" he asked Comfort. The blonde's expression was similar to biting into a persimmon. Mention of Elizabeth's name reminded Comfort that she had to fight for Slocum's attentions.

Slocum was past caring about such petty jealousies. He gathered canvas and whatever else he could from the wagon, then slung it over his trusty horse. The Arapaho pony reared and kicked at him. His numb fingers slid on the reins, and the horse ran off into the storm. Slocum let it go to die rather than futilely chase after it. Bending over against the wind, he led his horse and the mules up into the foothills where he had left Elizabeth. As he walked, he hunted for a larger cave that would house the lot of them. They would need all the heat they could muster over the night.

Elizabeth came from the cave and waved.

"Is there a bigger cave?" he called back. "One we can put the mules and horse inside?"

"I think so. Before the snow started blowing so, I saw a huge dark opening yonder." The brunette pointed into the whiteness even farther from the road. Slocum wished he could have scouted it out first, but there was no time. In spite of the other women's grumbling, he kept moving. He might have left them in the shallow cave with Elizabeth until he found better overnight quarters for them, but if he had done so, he might never have gotten back.

Every step now was a fight. The mules protested, and his horse slipped constantly on the slick ground. When he spotted the dark oval in the hillside, he hoped it was not simply dark rock decoying him to his death.

Slocum heaved a deep sigh when he saw the narrow, high-ceilinged cave led back into the hillside as far as he could see into the darkness. This was perfect for weathering the storm.

"Safe at last," Comfort said, pushing past him into the cave. "Here, I'll lead the mules inside and—" The blonde froze when a growl sounded from deeper inside the cave. "What was *that*?" she asked in a voice hardly loud enough to hear over the whistling wind.

Slocum drew the rifle from his saddle sheath and levered in a round. The Winchester's mechanism was sluggish from the cold. He should have cleaned all the oil off so it wouldn't freeze. Worse, he had no idea if the cold round resting in the firing chamber was going to go off when he fired—and fire he would have to.

They had found a cave already occupied by a bear.

"Stay here. Hang on to the animals," Slocum ordered.

"What's wrong?" called Maggie, hurrying up.

"You tell her," Slocum said to Comfort. He pushed past the mules and his horse and almost collapsed from relief when the cave walls blocked the wind against his face and body. He recovered quickly, squinting into the inky cave depths. Sniffing, he detected the gamy odor of a bear. He doubted the big brute would cotton much to sharing his quarters with a bunch of humans and their mules.

As cautious as he was, Slocum was taken by surprise when a section of cave wall suddenly reared and heavy claws slashed at his face. He threw up his hands to protect himself and lost his rifle. It crashed into the far wall, leaving him to face an angry bear with only his six-shooter.

Slocum knew a handgun might not bring down a bear this size. It wasn't big as bears went, but it was tough. Surviving along the Front Range with so many miners traveling over the pass told him that much. The Arapahos hunted here, and men on the road were always on the lookout for fresh meat. Fresh bear meat would suit just about any taste.

The bear snarled and lunged at Slocum again. He backpedaled and avoided another potentially deadly slash of the three-inch-long claws. The bear spun, then reared to take another swipe at him. This time Slocum had decided the time was ripe for fighting, not running.

He fired four rounds into the bear's exposed belly. Tiny red spots blossomed, but the pain enraged the bear. The bullets were hardly more than an annoyance to the large beast.

"My rifle!" Slocum cried. "Get it and shoot the bear." He didn't care who obeyed, as long as someone did. He backed deeper into the Stygian depths, less able to see by the second. The bear's large, furry body blotted out what little light came from the mouth of the cave.

He fired twice more, emptying his Colt Navy. Slocum had aimed for the heart but obviously missed. The bear growled angrily and lumbered forward, ready for dinner.

The bright flash and sharp report from his rifle stunned Slocum for a split second. Then he came to his senses, ducked and avoided another deadly swipe from the bear's claws. A second shot into the beast's back knocked it forward. From what Slocum could tell, the slug might have shattered the bear's spine. It kicked about feebly and roared in pain so loudly that even the storm wind played second fiddle.

Slocum danced past the thrashing bear and took the rifle from Rachel's steady hands. He aimed for the back of the bear's shaggy head and fired. This round stilled the animal permanently.

In spite of the cold, Slocum sweated like a pig. He wiped it from his forehead before it could freeze.

"Thanks," he said.

"You saved me from Kincannon. We're even now." Rachel spoke as though she dared him to argue the point. Slocum was past that. He felt only a flood of relief at being alive. Not many men blundered into a bear den and came out alive.

"Get the mules in here," Slocum said to Elizabeth and Comfort. "They'll be skittish because of the bear, but there's no way we can get rid of the scent." He tugged at the dead bear's legs, then heaved. He barely moved the body a few inches before giving up. To his surprise, Maggie and Rachel grabbed the bear's other hind leg. They pulled and grunted and finally got the bear into the mouth of the cave where the body could block more of the snow blowing in.

Slocum stared at the dead creature and wished he could skin it and get the bearskin for a blanket. There was no way. He had to make do with what was possible.

"The mules are settling down. Do we have to keep them in here with us?" asked Rachel.

"They'd freeze outside. Besides, their body heat'll help us as much as ours does them." He shivered in the cold again, moving deeper into the cave. He wished he could have foraged for wood, but to leave the cave now meant death. Even if he could have seen more than a few feet, the temperature was dropping like a rock. His coat wasn't up to the chore of keeping him warm.

Slocum slapped his hands against his arms and stamped his feet, hoping he wouldn't end up like Frosty. He wanted to keep his toes as long as he could.

"What was that all about?" Slocum asked Rachel.

"What are you talking about?"

"Kincannon. Why did he kidnap you along with Comfort and Maggie?"

"He was a son of a bitch, a real vulture."

"It was Elizabeth he wanted," Slocum said.

"Good riddance to him, that's what I say." And then Rachel said no more. She turned to huddle with the other three women. Slocum wasn't inclined to let the matter drop. He had killed two men and three others had died, taking Voss into account. And that didn't count however many Arapahos had died at Zacharias's hand. The women were like a tornado whirling along, leaving death and destruction all around them.

"The bounty hunter is still out there," Slocum said.

Comfort's eyes went wide. She opened her mouth to say something, but to Slocum's surprise it was Rachel who seemed the most rattled.

"I thought he was dead."

"He had me tied up, but I got away. When Elizabeth and I heard the shots, I thought it was Zacharias taking Comfort into custody. It never occurred to me that Kincannon was still on the trail."

"It was Kincannon," Rachel said. She chewed on her lower lip and looked at Slocum, her dark eyes unreadable. "The bounty hunter will die out there in the storm, won't he?"

"I don't know what happened to him," Slocum said. He had scant time to consider where Zacharias might have gone. Why hadn't he made a beeline directly to the women in the wagon? Something had waylaid him, but Slocum had come to believe the bounty hunter was unkillable. He had failed a couple times to kill Zacharias, as had the Arapahos. Maybe Kincannon had failed, too.

"We can't stay here," Rachel said, turning panicky. "We have to get to Leadville."

"Not until the storm passes," Slocum said. He looked into the white curtain and knew no one could survive more than a few feet in that blizzard. They didn't have the coats or boots for it, and it was colder than a witch's tit inside the cave. But here, they might ride out the storm.

"When we get out of here and get back to the wagon, I'll see you on the road to Leadville."

"It sounds like you're going to abandon us," Maggie said, looking as horror-struck as Rachel.

"The thought has crossed my mind," Slocum admitted. He was curious about the women and their headlong rush to get to Leadville, to find husbands, they said. From all he could tell, Elizabeth was running away from one—a dead one now, thanks to Slocum's quick six-shooter. His curiosity was rapidly wearing thin. How many more times did he have to cross Bear Zacharias?

"You can't do that!"

"You can come with me back to Denver," he said. "It's a free country."

"Slocum, no, that won't do. We *have* to go to Leadville." Maggie sounded desperate.

"Why? Afraid the silver strike will peter out and there won't be any rich miners left next spring? Keep on and you might die. Wait a few months and you might see all the riches you ever dreamed of."

"We'll pay you. A lot. Gold. Silver. You call it. No greenbacks. Hard metal."

"How much?" Slocum asked, his curiosity again coming into play. What was it worth to Maggie to get to Leadville.

"A hundred dollars." Maggie looked wild-eyed as she made the offer.

"I can make more than that selling the wagon and team."

"Five hundred."

Slocum's eyebrows rose, tiny hunks of ice falling off. Maggie hadn't upped the ante. Rachel had.

"You'll pay me five hundred in specie to see you to Leadville?"

"That's the deal," Rachel said.

"I'll think on it," Slocum said. "Right now, we ought to think on staying alive. And it might mean all of us cozying up to the mules."

They went deeper into the dark cave. Rachel and Maggie went off by themselves while Slocum found himself sandwiched between Elizabeth and Comfort under a pair of blankets. It ought to have been a pleasant way to spend the night, but Slocum eventually decided he knew how a deer felt being hunted by two wolves.

It was a long and virtually sleepless night for him.

18

Slocum looked out over the wintery blanket and had to squint. The bright sun had come up in a crystal-clear blue sky, belying the storm that had howled through most of the night. He stretched, his muscles sore and cramped. Now and again during the night either Comfort or Elizabeth would run her hands under his shirt and sometimes down into his pants, as if this would make him favor her over the other. Mostly, it had kept Slocum awake and lying uncomfortably in peculiar positions.

"Everyone out," Slocum called. "Back to the wagon so we can get food."

"And on the trail to Leadville?" asked Maggie.

"Yeah," Slocum said, damning himself for a fool. But the day was too beautiful for him to upbraid himself for long. They got back to the deserted wagon in less than fifteen minutes. While the women fixed a quick meal, Slocum went scouting for any trace of Bear Zacharias. The snow stretched in an unbroken white blanket as far as he could see. He considered returning to the bounty hunter's camp to see if Zacharias might be there, then discarded the notion. The best thing Slocum could do now was get in the wagon and drive.

But which way? He had told Maggie they'd be heading over Mosquito Pass, but it was his team and wagon and it rested on him to make the decisions to keep them alive. He could turn around and go back down to Denver.

"In for a penny, in for a dollar," he told himself. The notion Rachel had promised him five hundred dollars also goaded him to crossing the Front Range and reaching the boomtown soon.

In a half hour they were on the slick, icy road. In two hours the road had turned muddy from melting snow, but Slocum kept the mules pulling. By noon the next day they reached the summit and in another two days pulled into Leadville.

Slocum had spent as much time looking over his shoulder, wondering what had become of Zacharias, as he had watching the alternately icy and muddy road ahead. It came as a complete surprise to him when men scurried off as the wagon rattled along the sloppy road into town, only to return with a roaring crowd.

Along both sides of the main street men took off their hats and threw them in the air, cheering wildly.

"Lookee there," cried one man, bolder than the rest who had come up to peer into the back of the wagon. "I never seen such beauty in all my born days! Marry me!"

"Which one are you talking to?" asked Slocum, wondering if he ought to use the whip to drive the man back.

"Any of 'em. They're all real purty!"

Slocum kept the wagon rolling as others in the crowd elbowed past their partners to get a look at the four women. All of them preened and smiled and blew kisses until Slocum wanted to stop and warn them they were playing with dynamite. There might be a few women in town, but none was as lovely as Rachel, Maggie, Comfort or Elizabeth. Get the men heated up enough and there would be trouble.

"The hotel, Slocum, take us to the hotel," called Maggie.

That suited Slocum just fine. He reined back and stopped the mules so the women could jump onto the shabby boardwalk without getting their shoes dirty in the muddy street.

More than one miner offered to carry them in, but the women wisely refused. Slocum watched in wonder as the four entered the hotel as haughty as European royalty.

"Mister, any of them fillies yours?" asked one old-timer.

"Nope, I'm just the freighter," Slocum said.

"Good, cuz I got my eye on one of 'em." The miner cackled. "The one with red hair's a real looker."

"Don't know if they already have husbands lined up," Slocum said, remembering the letters he had found in Elizabeth's—and Comfort's—trunks.

"Don't matter. I kin outbid danged near anybody but old Tabor, and he's got his own filly." The miner reached into his pocket and pulled out a roll of greenbacks big enough to choke a cow. Mumbling to himself on how pretty he found Maggie, the filthy miner tromped into the hotel.

Slocum shook his head. The four women might have hit the mother lode, after all. But the price they'd pay for being wealthy struck Slocum as too high. He got the team moving toward the town's livery stable. Whatever the women did now was all their own doing. He had brought them to Leadville and would collect his money from Rachel later.

"Nice rig," the owner of the livery said. "You lookin' to sell?"

"Strange you ask," Slocum said, climbing down and starting the dickering. Voss's gambling debt was finally paid off, and Slocum was three hundred dollars richer. He might have gotten more, but he was getting itchy about riding on. The weather had cooperated the past few days and might shift at any time. Before the storms got bad, he needed to decide where to head. South, maybe as far as sunny, warm Mexico, appealed to him more as time went by.

First, he wanted to whet his whistle.

He had his choice of saloons. Slocum made his way through the mud to the saloon across the street from the hotel where he had left the women. The large crowd outside the hotel's front door told him it wasn't the right time to check on the women—or to collect his money from Rachel. Slocum was feeling downright sassy with so much money in his pocket as he went into the saloon to spend some of it.

"Whiskey," he said to the barkeep. "A bottle."

"Fifty bucks, mister," the bartender said. Slocum blinked. Boomtowns charged outrageous prices. He ought to have brought a case of whiskey in from Denver. He could have been rich.

"A shot, then," Slocum said. He swirled the amber liquor around in the shot glass for a while, sniffed appreciatively, then downed it. The burning all the way to his belly pleased him. As he sat the glass back on the bar, ready for another of the dollar drinks, he overheard two miners next to him swapping lies.

"Oh, yeah, you think *he* was big?" asked one. "I seen this fella outside o' town yesterday bigger 'n that. He was nuthin' but gristle and mean. Looked like a damned bear and smelt like one, too!"

The other miner countered with a gent he had seen in Denver, but Slocum turned to listen to the miner next to him going on about the man he had spotted the day before. The more the miner talked, the colder Slocum got inside.

"Tell me," Slocum asked. "You talk to this fellow? The one you said was the size of a bear?"

"Thass what he called hisself," the miner said. "Bear. He was huntin' for a woman, but then in these parts, who ain't?"

"A blonde?" interrupted Slocum.

The miner looked strangely at Slocum, then nodded. "How'd you know that?"

Slocum described Zacharias as carefully as he could.

"Thass the fella. You see him, too? Tell Ben here he lost our bet, that this fella's bigger 'n any three men!"

"You lose," Slocum said to Ben, hardly paying the man any mind. He asked the first man, "Where did you see Bear?"

Slocum wasted no time getting to his horse and heading out of town, backtracking to the road leading up into the pass. Somehow, Zacharias had gotten ahead of them, and Slocum had not picked up the man's trail as they drove into Leadville. The muddy road must have covered all signs of him preceding the wagon. Slocum neither knew nor cared what had happened to the bounty hunter on the other side of the pass before the storm. He had a score to settle, and it was best done before Zacharias knew that Slocum was in town.

Spotting four miners pulling a large cart, Slocum rode up and watched them for a moment. The cart was heaped with ore. Slocum was no expert, but the rock looked worthless.

"Taking it in for assay?" he asked the miners.

"We hit the mother lode," declared one miner. The other three glared at him, as if he gave away all the secrets of the universe. The man cleared his throat and added lamely, "Well, maybe."

"You see a huge guy on the road?" Slocum went on to describe Zacharias the best he could. From the way the four exchanged looks, he knew they had.

"Seems like we might have," another miner said cautiously. "What's it to you?"

"You might say he's my partner. We've done considerable business in the past." Slocum felt their hot eyes raking over the worn ebony butt of his Colt Navy, the cut of his clothing, the way he rode. Their attitude changed as they pegged him as another bounty hunter.

"Earlier in the day. Not a mile from here. Pitched camp that way," the first miner said.

"Good luck with your ore. Hope it assays out to five ounces a ton or better."

"Thanks, mister. You sound like you know your ore. What'cha think of this?" The other three miners jabbed him with elbows and frowned at him.

"Hard work is its own reward," Slocum said, putting his heels to his horse and trotting away. He doubted they would find anything valuable at their claim, but perhaps they did not have to. Small bits of silver arduously plucked from the rock might give them enough money to live on, if not get rich.

Slocum veered off the road when he saw a curl of white smoke ahead, about where the four miners had spotted Zacharias on their way to town. Dismounting, Slocum drew his six-gun and checked to be sure all the chambers were loaded. The bounty hunter had taken incredible punishment in the past. The bear in the cave reminded him a great deal of Zacharias, taking four slugs from the six-shooter, then two more from a rifle before dying.

He intended to end Zacharias's life using only his six-shooter.

Slocum came on the campfire from the east. This might allow Zacharias an easy way out, but it also afforded Slocum the chance to sneak up on him. The bounty hunter watched the road and not his back, sitting and staring at the nearby muddy ruts that passed for road.

Zacharias sat erect, his hands going for the shotgun beside him when Slocum cocked his six-shooter.

"Don't," Slocum said. "I'm no backshooter, but I'm not

giving you the chance to get that scattergun up and firing, either."

"Slocum!"

"What's it take to kill you, Zacharias?" Slocum's trigger finger twitched. A single slow pull would send a bullet into the back of the bounty hunter's head. It would be over. All over. And Slocum wouldn't have any answers to questions burning away at him.

"More gravel 'n you got, Slocum."

"Don't push your luck. How much is the reward on Comfort?"

"The blonde whore?"

Slocum fired, his slug ripping off a piece of Zacharias's ear. The bounty hunter yelped in pain and grabbed for the bleeding crease.

"You keep a civil tongue in your head or I'll cut it out," Slocum snapped. "How much was the reward?"

"Two hundred dollars. Gold. Ought to be more. Ought to be a thousand."

"For what crime?"

"You been screwin' her, Slocum. Didn't she tell ya?"

"How dead do you want to be in ten seconds, Zacharias?"

"The warrant's for murder. Back in Saint Loo. She done upped and kilt some banker fellow. Shot him. Probably deserved it, but that's not what the law says."

"What about the others with Comfort? You after them, too?"

"For what? I ain't got reward posters on them. What they done, Slocum? You fixin' to make a deal with me? We round 'em all up and split the reward? Well, I ain't gonna do it! I tracked that blonde bitch all the way across Kansas and—"

Zacharias yelped again when Slocum fired. This shot ripped away some of the thinning hair on the top of his head.

"Watch what you call those ladies," Slocum said, although he agreed more with Zacharias's estimation than he cared to admit.

"Awright, awright. Them ladies ain't of no interest to me. They're way too skinny fer the likes of me, anyhow. But the blonde one. She's worth money, if 'n I get her to a federal marshal."

Slocum considered this. Leadville was a boomtown. It might have a sheriff or a city marshal—the town fathers probably insisted on a minimal amount of law. But there wasn't likely to be a federal marshal this side of the Front Range. Zacharias had to take Comfort back to Denver if he wanted his reward.

"The storms will close Mosquito Pass before long."

"I'll keep her tied up all winter long, if I have to. Nobody does me out of my reward, Slocum. Nobody, and that includes you!"

Zacharias was not subtle, but he moved like greased lightning. He dived for his shotgun. Slocum reacted before he even knew what was going on. His bullet sent the shotgun spinning from Zacharias' grasp. The next round was meant to kill, but the bounty hunter's reactions were snakelike in their speed.

The bullet that had been aimed for the middle of his forehead missed by a couple inches.

Zacharias grunted and then his eyes rolled up into his head. He fell over like a giant Pacific Coast redwood being sawed down. He lay on the cold ground, unconscious.

Slocum cocked his Colt again, ready for the shot that would eliminate the bounty hunter from his life forever. Then he lowered the hammer and put his six-shooter back into his cross-draw holster. He was no cold-blooded killer. Shooting Zacharias in a fight was one thing. Gunning him down when he was knocked out was something else.

As much as Slocum wanted, he couldn't kill the bounty hunter outright. Too many men had already died around the four women, and Slocum was getting sick of too much spilled blood.

Slocum went to the bounty hunter's side and rolled him onto his back. Then he hog-tied Zacharias so the man wouldn't get free for a week. If he starved, so be it, but Slocum reckoned someone would come along before then and set him free.

A dirty rag served as a gag. Then Slocum rummaged through Zacharias's saddlebags, hunting for the wanted posters he was sure the bounty hunter carried. He found them, a dozen or more. The top one showed a crude likeness of Comfort.

"Comfort Tomasson," he mused. Slocum had never heard her last name. Or the last names of any of the other three women, for that matter. It had never seemed too important. He searched the pile of wanted posters, but the rest were of men. Zacharias had told the truth that Comfort was the only one with a price on her head.

Slocum stuffed the wad of posters under his belt, then checked his knots to be sure that Zacharias was securely tied. No wiggling calf could get free the way Slocum had fastened the ropes.

It was time to go collect his money from Maggie—and then see what made the women run.

19

It was close to noon when Slocum rode back into Lead-ville. He hardly believed his eyes at the size of the line curling out the front doors of the hotel. It was as though the circus had come to town and all the kids lined up to buy tickets to see the elephants and clowns.

A cold knot growing in his belly, Slocum dismounted and approached a man waiting impatiently at the end of the line.

"What's the occasion?" Slocum asked. He got the answer he had suspected.

"Women," the man said eagerly. "They're takin' applications for husbands. Three of the best-lookin' ladies you ever seen, and they've come here to Leadville!" The man bounced a bag of coins. Slocum silently pointed to it. The man said, "Application fee. I'm sure to get one of 'em, no matter how many're ahead of me. I got more 'application fee' than any of them others."

Slocum shrugged, then stopped and thought what the man had said. Three ladies? He went around to the rear of the hotel and slipped into the kitchen. A cook looked up at him and brandished a meat cleaver.

"You git on back out there now wit' the rest of them bums. No sneakin' in!"

"I brought the women to Leadville from Denver," Slocum said.

"That don't make you special. Git on out of my kitchen!"

Slocum ducked around the irate woman and into the dining room. He stared at the arrangement. Elizabeth, Maggie and Comfort had set up at different parts of the table, stacks of paper in front of each. Across the table from each of the women sat a nervous miner being "interviewed."

Comfort looked up and saw Slocum. She smiled brightly and waved. The man she was taking money from glared, then quickly changed his attitude when Comfort leaned over the table and gave him a quick peck on the cheek before hustling him out so the next one could come.

Slocum sidled closer and watched as Elizabeth filled out the forms. He noted she did not write down names or descriptions, only the amount of gold dust or silver coins taken in. A quick sum told him Elizabeth had accounted for more than two thousand dollars already. He didn't doubt Maggie and Comfort had matched this amount on their own, if not surpassing it. Most of the miners seemed stricken when they saw Comfort's blond beauty, and Maggie brusquely moved her potential beaus through with mechanical efficiency.

"Where's Rachel?" he asked Elizabeth. The brunette did not bother looking up as she rapidly counted through a leather pouch presented her by the next man in her line.

"She's off taking care of some personal business. If you'll excuse me, John, I have to hurry along if I want to finish before sundown. It wouldn't do keeping any of these . . . worthy suitors waiting." She graced the miner sitting on the edge of his chair with a big smile.

Slocum wondered what was significant about finishing the interview process by sundown but hesitated to ask. He wondered if any of these men was the letter writer who had courted Elizabeth long-distance. Slocum knew better than to interrupt what was a booming business on the part of the three women.

He pushed past the lines of men rather than return through the kitchen and the harpy fixing dinner there. If anything, the lines were longer than before. It wouldn't surprise Slocum if the three women raked in ten thousand dollars each by the time they quit for the day. What were they going to do with the money from rejected suitors?

The cold knot in Slocum's belly turned harder and colder. He had the urge to get on his horse and ride like hell to get as far away from Leadville as he could. Slocum was not sure what was going on, but the fat would be in the fire soon, and he didn't want to be near enough to get spattered.

He ought to have ridden out, but too many questions went unanswered. Why wasn't Rachel with the other three? And there was the matter of the would-be husband Elizabeth had written to, keeping all the letters in her trunk. Slocum thought hard and remembered the name: Hamilton.

He went to a miner in the line and accosted him. "You know a miner named Hamilton?" he asked.

The man looked startled, then bobbed his head up and down like it was on a spring.

"Sure, mister, everyone knows Pete Hamilton. Danged near the most successful mine owner in these parts."

"Where might I find him?"

"Out at the Ragin' Rachel Mine. Got a vein of silver a yard wide. I worked for him a spell and seen it with my own eyes. Then I got my own mine. The Glory Bee."

"That way out of town?" Slocum asked, pointing. He got more detailed directions and headed for the oddly named mine. Signs along the road directed him into the foothills, where mine shafts dug deep into the rock and left tailings like dark vomit down the hillside. Slocum noticed that no one seemed to be working the mine today and wondered if Hamilton had given his men the day off to go find themselves wives.

The thought struck Slocum as funny and he laughed. Then he stopped when he saw the horse and buggy pulled up behind a line shack. Another horse, this one saddled, strained at its tether to get free. The reason for its skittishness became apparent when a shriek of pure agony rang out. Slocum had heard men tortured before, by Apaches and even by soldiers he had ridden with during the war. This horrific sound carried all the pain and misery of a terrible world.

Slocum hit the ground and drew his six-gun. He advanced to the side of the shack and chanced a look in through a broken window at the side. For a moment he stood, not sure he had seen what he did. Slocum looked again, this time taking more time to study the two people in the cabin and what was happening.

The coldness in his belly turned to a rock the size of Pike's Peak. He quickly went around the shack, braced himself, then kicked the door open.

Rachel looked up, a crazed expression on her bloodspattered face. She held a thin-bladed surgical knife she had used expertly on the man tied up on the floor.

"Slocum!"

"Drop it, Rachel."

She snarled like a savage wild animal and came at him. If he hesitated a fraction of a second, he knew he would be gutted and writhing on the shack's dirt floor. His Colt Navy spat death. The slug caught Rachel in the center of the chest, right between her breasts. The small caliber bullet killed her but did not stop her maniacal advance. Although dead, she came on, the blade held high and ready to slay.

Stepping to one side, Slocum let the woman stumble

past and crash facedown to the ground outside. The knife remained clenched in her fist.

"Oh, god, on, god, I *hurt* so bad," the man moaned.

Slocum had seen men blown apart on the battlefield but seldom had he seen anything this bloody or stomach-turning.

"I'll do what I can for you. Did . . . did Rachel do this?" The question came out involuntarily. It wasn't time to interrogate the man; it was time to do what he could to save him. And barring that, put him out of his misery as he would any injured animal that would suffer needlessly.

"Yes, yes, she did. Can't believe it. My own wife . . ."

Slocum didn't bother pursuing the matter. He got a kettle of water boiling, then settled down to strip the bloody clothing off the man to find the worst of the wounds. He stanched the flow from a few small arteries that had been severed, but for the most part the man had suffered mightily with little permanent damage.

Slocum shuddered when he remembered the book in Rachel's carpetbag. An anatomy book. She had studied how best to torture this man.

"You're Hamilton?"

"C-call me Pete," the man said. "Most folks do."

The boiling water came in handy, cleaning the wounds and locating a few more spurting arteries Rachel had severed. Slocum used a red-hot poker to cauterize Hamilton's wounds.

"She must have hated you something fierce," Slocum observed.

"She—she did. Might be Rachel had good reason, but to do this to me . . ." Hamilton shuddered.

"The Ragin' Rachel—you named your mine after her?"

"I did. I loved her, but she wouldn't come out here with me. Wanted to stay in Denver."

"So you started courting Elizabeth?" Slocum asked, a glimmering of what had happened coming to him.

"How'd you know?" Hamilton's eyes widened in surprise. "You're not Elizabeth's husband, are you? She said she was trying to get away from him and—"

"I killed him," Slocum said bitterly. Pete Hamilton turned pale when Slocum admitted to Walt Kincannon's death. "Don't worry about it. Elizabeth's nothing to me."

"I don't understand Rachel. She wouldn't divorce me, but she wouldn't come here, either. Except to torture me."

Slocum wondered if Elizabeth had started the long-distance romance with Hamilton at Rachel's request. It might have been a tit-for-tat deal so they could both get rid of unwanted husbands. But Rachel's hatred went past most women's for a man they wanted rid of.

She had been plumb loco the way she had planned and executed Hamilton's torture. And he had seen her face as she was carving the man up. What worried Slocum most was the chance he might never be able to get that demented expression out of his worst nightmares.

"I'd forget all about Rachel—and Elizabeth," Slocum suggested, beginning the chore of binding Hamilton's wounds so he could travel. Leadville had to have a sawbones capable of sewing up the deeper knife cuts. Hamilton's face and torso would be criss-crossed with scars for the rest of his life, but he was alive.

Slocum swallowed hard when he thought what Rachel would have done to the mine owner if she had gotten down below his waist. Sometimes, it's better off being dead.

"I'll swear off all women for all time," Hamilton said.

"There's a buggy outside. Rachel must have come out from town in it. You up to traveling? You need a doctor pretty bad," Slocum said.

"I'm kinda cold. And weak as a kitten, but yeah, let's go. I want to get away from here." Hamilton tried to stand on his own and failed. Slocum carried him out to the buggy. The man's eyes flickered open and a half-smile came to his lips. "I'm gonna change the mine's name. To The Lucky SOB."

"Good choice," Slocum said, getting in after he had hitched his and Hamilton's horses to the back of the buggy. Somewhere halfway into town, Hamilton passed out, but Slocum got him to the doctor's surgery where the sawbones could do his damnedest. It even looked as if Hamilton would live by the time Slocum stepped out onto Leadville's main street.

The sun had gone down and the night air had turned frigid. The altitude made Slocum huff and puff as he walked toward the hotel. He needed to talk to Elizabeth, Comfort and Maggie about Rachel. He saw now how Rachel had been the leader, getting them involved in her scheme to come to Leadville so she could kill her cheating husband.

It didn't make much difference, but Slocum thought Rachel might have put Elizabeth up to sparking the exchange of love letters with Pete Hamilton to give herself a reason to vent her insane anger on the man.

That Elizabeth had to flee from her own husband figured into it—she went along with Rachel to get away from Kincannon. But what was the point of breezing into Leadville, pretending they were virgins auditioning for husbands?

"Fire!" went up the cry. Slocum sprinted down the street toward the hotel. Already men struggled to get pumps and hoses unrolled while others wrestled water barrels nearer the blazing hotel. As in any boomtown, the fear of fire was ever present and deservedly so. The wood used to build most structures was tinder dry. Putting the buildings close together made a small fire turn into a city-devouring conflagration if the volunteer firemen didn't act fast.

From inside the hotel came screams rivaling anything Slocum had heard Pete Hamilton utter.

"Who's still inside?" Slocum asked one would-be fireman who was almost too drunk to stand.

"Don't know. Dozen folks, maybe more. And them women. The women's in there, men!"

This spurred the firemen to extraordinary effort. Slocum stepped back as the screams from inside died along with the people trapped in the hotel. He turned, the heat of the raging fire at his back. It took him a few minutes to find that the wagon he and the women had driven over Mosquito Pass was missing, along with the team of mules. He mounted his horse and considered directions.

There was no point going north into the snow and cold. Earlier, he had thought about heading south toward Cripple Creek and Victor and then down toward Mexico. That struck him as the road to take now.

Less than a half hour brought him to a rise where he could look down over the next few miles of road. Rattling along in the dark, mules straining to pull the heavy wagon, he saw Elizabeth, Maggie and Comfort. He sucked in his breath, then released it slowly, wheeled about and galloped for the far side of Leadville.

The hotel fire had been put out. Charred bodies were being removed as he rode past. The stench turned his stomach almost as much as the knowledge of whom had set the fire and why.

Slocum rode until he found the spot where he had left Bear Zacharias tied up. The bounty hunter still fought mindlessly against the ropes. He looked up, hatred brimming in his eyes when he saw Slocum.

The first words from his mouth when Slocum plucked out the gag were, "You come back to taunt me, Slocum? I swear, I—"

"Shut up or I'll stuff the gag back in. You listen and you listen good. I'm going to do you a favor."

"What? Why?"

"You want a big reward? A *really* big one?"

"Who do I have to kill?"

"Nobody," Slocum said, suddenly bone-tired. He sat on a rock and considered what he was doing. Then his resolve hardened. "You ride along the road to the south leading out of Leadville. You'll find Comfort in a wagon. Don't just take her back to Leadville. Take the other two, also. Maggie's the redhead and Elizabeth has brown hair."

"Why? I ain't got no posters on them."

"Take the three back to Leadville and let the law know you're returning the women who robbed a passel of miners with a fake marriage swindle. And who murdered a dozen or more people by setting a fire in the hotel to cover their tracks."

"I don't get it. Why you doin' this?"

"I've got enough blood on my hands," Slocum said. He sliced through the ropes holding the bounty hunter. Zacharias glared at him, then stomped off toward Leadville. Slocum knew there would be three nooses for three lovely necks swinging from a cottonwood before long.

He didn't want to be around when the women were hanged.

He mounted his horse and started out on the road again, this time heading in the opposite direction. It promised only storm and freezing cold to the north, but that suited Slocum just fine now. Before midnight, he rode into the teeth of a new blizzard that seemed almost peaceable after all he had been through with the four deadly, delectable women.

J. R. ROBERTS
THE
GUNSMITH